LINKED

LOOK FOR MORE ACTION AND HUMOR FROM
GORDON KORMAN

War Stories

Restart

Whatshisface

Slacker

Level 13

Radio Fifth Grade

The Toilet Paper Tigers

The Chicken Doesn't Skate

This Can't Be Happening at Macdonald Hall!

THE HYPNOTISTS SERIES
The Hypnotists
Memory Maze
The Dragonfly Effect

THE SWINDLE SERIES
Swindle
Zoobreak
Framed
Showoff
Hideout
Jackpot
Unleashed
Jingle

The Titanic trilogy

The Kidnapped trilogy

The On the Run series

The Dive trilogy

The Everest trilogy

The Island trilogy

LINKED

GORDON KORMAN

SCHOLASTIC PRESS / NEW YORK

Library Congress Cataloging-in-Publication Data available

ISBN 978-1-338-62911-8

1 2021

Printed in the U.S.A.   23
First edition, July 2021

Book design by Yaffa Jaskoll

FOR JONATHAN GREENBLATT
THANKS FOR YOUR GUIDANCE AND SUPPORT

CHAPTER ONE

MICHAEL AMOROSA

My mother says I'd lose my head if it wasn't attached to my body.

Too bad my phone isn't also attached somewhere. I left it at school again. I know this because it butt-dialed our landline at home. I have no idea why. Ever since I dropped it in the toilet, it's been glitchy.

When I pick up, I hear a muffled motor in the background. I'm hoping that means the phone is in my locker and the noise is Mr. Kennedy, the custodian, using the big floor-polishing machine. Then the sound dies abruptly. That either means Mr. Kennedy finished polishing or my phone died. It's super old, so a battery charge lasts a millionth of a second.

I jump on my bike. Chokecherry is a pretty small town, but we live on the opposite side, so it's a long ride. I'm used to it, though. I always leave something at school, and nine times out of ten, I have to go back and get it. Mom and Dad would give me a lift, but then they'd *know*.

"I'm going out" is all the detail I provide.

Thanks to the new security, every single door to the school is locked. But I still go from entrance to entrance, banging and yelling, hoping that Mr. Kennedy is close enough to one of them to hear me over the roar of the polisher. To my surprise, the door to the boys' locker room swings open when I kick it. I'm in.

I'm entering the school from the back corner that leads out to the football field, but my locker is in the main hall, not far from the principal's office. The floor polisher sounds far away, maybe upstairs.

I open my locker, and there it is, the world's oldest phone. I probably shouldn't have called it eleven times, because it's sitting on a tray of poster paints, and all that vibrating has made the blue and yellow leak out together, raining green blobs down on my geography textbook. I'm president of the art club, so I've always got supplies in my locker—and stains on my gym clothes, books, etc. Last year, I got charged a fifty-dollar cleaning fee to remove the melted pastel from my iPad screen. Like it's my fault the temperature went up to a hundred the weekend before the last day of school.

I check the phone. Dead. Just like I suspected. I shut my locker and turn to leave.

Only I don't leave. I freeze.

I blink and blink again, struggling to wrap my mind around what I'm seeing.

It's spray-painted in red on the blank expanse of wall above the staircase leading to the second story—that large X with each arm continued at a right angle.

I stare at it in horror and disbelief, hoping that my eyes are deceiving me and this ugly red symbol is something other than what I know it is.

A swastika.

"Michael?"

Mr. Kennedy's voice startles me out of my state of shock. I drop my phone, which bounces on the floor. It's probably cracked, possibly ruined, but I can't tear my gaze from the symbol on the wall.

"What did you forget this time?" the custodian asks in exasperation.

All I can do is point up. When Mr. Kennedy sees it, a sharp gasp is torn from him.

He turns to me. "You didn't—" he begins. "I mean, you wouldn't—"

"Of course not!" I answer. Why would the only Dominican kid in the whole school be the one to draw a racist symbol? I almost add, "Nobody would." But there's the evidence right in front of us.

Somebody *did*.

I reach down to pick up my phone and almost drop it again. The screen is fractured. But even through the spiderweb of damage, I can see that awful thing on the wall reflected in the glass.

The custodian takes out his own phone. "I'm calling the police."

CHAPTER TWO

LINCOLN ROWLEY

Let's get one thing straight: None of this would have happened if it wasn't for dinosaur poop.

I'm not making excuses for myself or anybody else. But way back in the Jurassic period, some Stegosaurus went to the bathroom in our mountains. And a hundred million years later, Jordie Duros, Clayton Pouncey, and I are teetering across a darkened parking lot, struggling under the weight of an eighty-pound bag.

"Are you sure this is the right stuff?" I pant as the bag passes under the glow of the streetlamp. "It says peat moss mix, not fertilizer."

"What if it doesn't stink?" Pouncey worries.

"Trust me, when we open the bag, we'll have more stink than we know what to do with," Jordie assures us. "My mom topped the cedar hedge with this stuff three weeks ago. I'm still sleeping with my windows closed."

It's a cool night, but carrying the heavy sack has us grunting and sweating like pigs.

The girls are waiting for us in front of the office.

"What took you so long?" Sophie Tavener complains. "We're freezing here!"

"Try carrying this," I groan. "It'll warm you right up."

The sign on the door reads:

WEXFORD-SMYTHE UNIVERSITY
DEPARTMENT OF PALEONTOLOGY

Why does a snooty college in Massachusetts have an office more than two thousand miles away, in Chokecherry, Colorado? That's where the dinosaur poop comes in. This is where they found it, all neatly fossilized. It looks like a rock, but don't you believe it. First they found the poop. Then they found a footprint in the poop. Dinosaurs weren't too picky where they stepped. So the college sent a crew to investigate. And when the first bone fragments popped up, that was it. They say the scientists will be here for years. A few of their kids even go to our school.

The digging is happening in the mountains, but the university opened up this little office in town so the PhDs can have a home base and also rub it in our faces how much smarter they are than us locals. The prank is my idea, inspired by a comment from Pouncey. Basically, if you get your jollies crawling on your hands and knees digging up fossilized poop, then you'll really love an office full of the real thing—smell included.

"Who brought the funnel?" Pouncey asks the girls.

"I did." Pamela Bynes holds up one of those plastic cooking funnels. The opening is maybe an eighth of an inch.

"Aw, Pam!" Jordie explodes. "There's no way we can get eighty pounds of fertilizer through that thing!"

Even in the gloom, I can see her face flame red. "You just said funnel! You didn't say *big* funnel—"

"It's fine," I interrupt. Once Pamela and Jordie start flirt-fighting, it can go on for hours. They've been like that since we were all seven—true love, I guess. It's usually pretty entertaining, but not when you're carrying an eighty-pound load.

Shifting the weight of the bag to my left hand, I tear a four-inch hole in the corner with my right. Instantly, the overpowering smell of manure reaches all our nostrils.

Pamela wrinkles her nose. "That stinks!"

"It's poop, Pam, not roses," Jordie snaps at her.

Sophie holds open the mail slot, and we insert our makeshift spout. Then we hold the bag high, tilt it, and begin shaking it until we feel the fertilizer starting to pour out.

Pamela produces a three-by-five card that reads *DINOSAUR POOP* and stuffs it in through the slot. "Just in case they don't get the joke," she supplies.

"They're scientists," Jordie says impatiently. "They're smart. They'll get it."

"They just might not appreciate it," I add with as much of a grin as I can manage under the circumstances.

"They're not so smart," Pouncey scoffs. "What's a diploma? A fancy piece of paper. That's what my dad says." He talks about his father a lot, which is weird, since the two of them can barely stand each other.

"I brought this." Sophie reaches into her jacket pocket and produces the wishbone from a medium-size chicken. "Wexford-Smythe didn't get really excited until they found bones." She stuffs the "fossil" in through the mail slot.

That makes us all laugh, even Pouncey, who isn't known for his sense of humor.

Since our eyes are adjusted to the darkness, when the car turns into the parking lot, the headlights are blinding. We pull the fertilizer bag out of the door, but there's no hiding it. We're caught in the act, lit up like performers on a stage.

Jordie bellows, "Run!"

"No—" I gasp.

I'm too late. They all take off, leaving me literally holding the bag. Maybe ten or fifteen pounds went in through the slot. The rest of it collapses on top of me. My head strikes the pavement, and I see a few stars that are not necessarily in the sky.

I hear a car door and running feet. By the time I manage to roll out from under the sack and make it up to my knees, a man is gazing down at me in concern.

"You okay, kid? What stinks?"

I try to say *I'm fine*, but the wind has been knocked out of me by at least sixty-five pounds of fertilizer.

"I told you the dry cleaner was closed," calls a woman's voice from the car. She pauses. "Hey, isn't that George Rowley's boy?"

Busted.

The problem with living in a one-horse town like Chokecherry is you can't get away with anything. Especially when your dad is George Rowley, owner of Chokecherry Real Estate, the largest—and the only—real estate agency in Chokecherry and greater Shadbush County.

He loves this town. More, I think, than he loves his trouble-making son.

Which is why I became the mastermind behind Operation Dino-doo-doo.

Even though five of us pulled the prank at the strip mall, I was the one who didn't have the luxury of taking off—not after that lady recognized me. Everybody around here knows my father. He's kind of like the stealth mayor—although Mayor Radisson has nothing to worry about. Dad doesn't have time for local politics. He's too busy being Chokecherry's number one cheerleader because, as he puts it, "the town's success brings success to all of us."

No wonder he's ticked off at me. Not only did I make fun of the town's pride and joy, but I was also a failure at doing it.

Story of my life.

"How do you think it feels, Link," Dad demands once he has me in the SUV, "when I get a call from one of my own clients to tell me my son has been caught vandalizing an office?"

"Everybody around here is your client," I point out. "So if you want the call to be from a stranger, I'll have to take the bus to Shadbush Crossing and mess up there."

"*Link,*" my mother warns from the shotgun seat. I call her The Referee. "You're the one who's in the wrong. What were you thinking?"

"He obviously *wasn't* thinking," my father puts in. "Or none of us would be here right now."

"I guess we thought it would be funny," I offer lamely. It's the truth. There are no bigger jokers in Chokecherry than Jordie, Pouncey, and me—with the girls as backup. To be honest, considering the time we spend pranking and goofing, we don't spend that much time *laughing*. Getting caught doesn't help, I guess.

That's okay. For me, the real goal is getting the attention of people like Dad.

Mission accomplished—although maybe not the way I'd planned.

Thinking of the others, I quickly amend my answer to "*I thought it would be funny.*" I'm no snitch . . . even though my friends ran out on me.

Mom shoots me an exasperated look over her shoulder. "Don't even bother. We aren't stupid, you know. One kid can't drag an eighty-pound bag of fertilizer halfway across town. Who was with you?"

I don't answer, and Dad doesn't push it. Trust me, he isn't being cool, or respecting the code of the schoolyard. He really, truly doesn't care who else is involved. All he's worried about is how this looks. *Optics.* It's his favorite word—after *chokecherry*. Leave it to our town to be named after a wild berry sour enough to change your outlook on life, with a pit the size of a cannonball.

Dad wheels us onto Blossom Avenue. "I'm not as out of touch as you think I am. I was a kid once too. I know sometimes you have to cut loose. But why that office, huh? The one group that's working to put Chokecherry on the map?"

That's the real reason Dad's so steamed about this. His main ambition in life is to turn our dumpy little mountain town into an A-list tourist destination. How's it going to happen? In a word: *dinosaurs.*

If the Wexford-Smythe paleontologists are right and our little dig turns into a major find, Dad wants to reinvent Chokecherry as the dinosaur capital of North America. First a museum full of towering skeletons surrounding a special glass case displaying the poop that started it all. Next a theme park— Dino-Disney or Six Flags Dino-land. Then hotels, restaurants, ski resorts, golf courses. Our town is destined for greatness, and the real estate in it is destined for greatness too. Guess who bought up most of it? And if Dino-land turns out to be a bust, guess who owns thirteen thousand acres of nothing?

"Chokecherry's already on the map," I say. "Why do we need scientists to make us important? I go to school with their kids, and they're all snobs and dweebs. Whoever heard of their stupid university anyway?"

"You know what Orlando, Florida, was before Disney found it?" my father persists. "A swamp. Look at it now. Chokecherry could be the next Orlando!"

"Too much traffic," Mom puts in.

Dad ignores her. "You have to think big picture, Link. The future of the town is the future of this family. And the future of this family is *your* future!"

I tune him out. If there's a word Dad likes almost as much as *optics,* it's *future.* In his mind, my entire life is this gigantic chess match, where every tiny move I make in the seventh grade has to be perfectly designed to bring about some glorious endgame decades later. When Jordie, Pouncey, and I spread lard across the Fourth of July parade route, we were just trying to wipe out the marching band. How were we supposed to know that semi was going to skid into a telephone pole? And when Dad banned me from all school sports teams as punishment, it wasn't for plunging the whole town into darkness for three days. It was "to protect your future."

There was no point in describing to him how awesome it was going to be to watch the musicians floundering all over the intersection. My father has the sense of humor of a loaf of bread. There was even less point in explaining that taking me out of sports would be like pulling him off the Chokecherry Chamber of Commerce. I mean, I'm a pretty popular kid, but if you ask people around here about Link Rowley, the main answer you get will be "Athlete."

Dad thinks if he just keeps slamming me with punishment after punishment, I'll wise up. The truth is I've wised up already—to *him*.

Mom sighs her peacemaker sigh. "Let's not fight. The sooner we can get this bag of fertilizer out to the shed, the sooner we can hose out the trunk."

Dad grunts his assent and speeds up a little. We're stopped at a light when his phone rings. When he answers, we hear a lot of animated yelling on the other end of the line. Suddenly, he stomps on the gas and we blow the light, screech through an illegal U-turn, and then blow the light in the opposite direction as we roar off down the road.

"George!" Mom hangs on to the dashboard for dear life. "Where are you going?"

"That was Principal Brademas," he replies grimly, leaning on the gas pedal. "There's trouble at the school."

CHAPTER THREE

DANA LEVINSON

The kids around here don't think I see them staring at me, but I do.

As I make my way up the front walk to Chokecherry Middle School, heads turn in my direction and animated conversations break out.

I'm used to being the new kid. Dad's work for Wexford-Smythe University has brought us to dinosaur digs all over the world. But Chokecherry is different. It isn't so much that it's small; it's *isolated*. The nearest big city, Denver, is a four-hour drive. Even Shadbush Crossing—the county seat—is almost a hundred miles away.

So the kids in Chokecherry all grew up together—like from the cradle. Where does that leave me? Out in the cold. By the time I show up in the middle of sixth grade, all the friend groups have been set for years.

I sort of understand. I don't even mind that much. But I've lived here for six months already . . . isn't it time I stopped being such a curiosity? They don't have to love me; I just wish they'd stop looking at me like I was a three-legged coyote that limped in from the mountains.

Maybe I'm being paranoid, but it feels like it's even worse

today. As I enter the building, they're gathered in small groups, peering at me and whispering. What's going on?

The main atrium is more crowded than usual. Mr. Brademas, the principal, is urging everyone to move on to their lockers, but nobody's budging. They're all gazing up at a gigantic beige tarp that's been duct-taped to the wall. Two custodians are perched on the stairs, working furiously behind the billowing sheet with long-handled mops. Red-stained water is trickling down and puddling on the floor.

I blurt, "Is that *blood*?"

Andrew Yee, an eighth grader whose mother works with Dad at the dinosaur dig, takes my arm and starts leading me out of the atrium. "Come on, Dana. Nothing to see here."

I shake him off. "Are they putting up a mural?"

"Nah," he replies. "They're just cleaning."

At that moment, the duct tape separates from the plaster, and the tarp peels away and drops to the floor. I stare at the wall that's now revealed.

I gawk. I goggle.

The lines have been blurred by the custodians' mops, but it's very clear what someone has painted up there. As I gaze in shock at the swastika in the atrium, it occurs to me that I've never seen one firsthand before. Oh, sure, in World War II movies and in books about the Nazis and the Holocaust. But not in my school, in a spot where six hundred kids walk under it every day. It's uglier up there than it looks on a page or a screen because it's not a picture or a prop. It's not there to help tell a story or to educate. It's the real thing, painted in anger and hatred.

Hundreds of phones appear, and the air fills with the whirring and snapping of pictures. I'm rooted to the spot. Now I understand what all the watching and whispering was about. A swastika is a symbol of hate in general, but it's especially a symbol of anti-Semitism. And everybody knows that I'm the only Jewish kid at Chokecherry Middle School.

I've never seen Mr. Brademas move quite so fast as he does getting over to the fallen tarp and handing it up to the custodians on the stairs. While they try to stick it back on the wall, the principal orders us to our homerooms.

Nobody moves. What we've just seen is awful, but for some reason we can't turn our backs on it.

"Put those phones away!" Mr. Brademas orders, sounding a lot like a Marine drill sergeant barking commands at new recruits. "Clear the atrium!"

At that point, the bell rings, and we all begin to shuffle off to lockers and homerooms. Behind us, the tarp hits the floor again, and I catch one more glimpse of *it* as I round the corner.

"You okay?" Andrew asks anxiously.

"Why wouldn't I be?" I snap.

And I *am* okay, I tell myself. Why should I get upset just because some wing nut put a swastika on the wall? I've been alive for thirteen years. It's not like this is the only bad thing I've ever seen. And this isn't Nazi Germany just because somebody painted a Nazi symbol.

I scan the faces in the hall. Most kids are talking a mile a minute about what we've just witnessed. One thing about a small town like Chokecherry: Nothing ever happens. So when it does, it's big news. A few people look kind of solemn and tight-lipped, but most have their phones out and are comparing swastika pictures. A few have even taken selfies with the awful thing in the background. Probably by the end of homeroom, Instagram will be flooded with the postings—*Me with swastika*. Cute.

Not cute.

Actually, deeply disturbing.

Okay, maybe I'm a little more rattled than I'm willing to admit. Because that swastika means there could be someone in this school who *hates* me. Not *dislikes* me, or finds me annoying. A swastika sends you directly to the h-word, do not pass Go, do not collect $200.

I've gotten strange looks in the past. A handful of insensitive, mean comments. But not hate. Nothing like that.

The swastika is bad enough, but the thought of some shadowy person actually *drawing* one is worse. Why would anybody do that? It's probably just a sick joke, but what if there's more to it than that?

If this question sends a chill up my spine, it seems to thrill a lot of my classmates. I can't believe that so many of them think this is a fun thing to spice up a boring school week—like the time the bus broke down and they had to call the giant tow truck. Excited speculation buzzes through the halls. Who did it? And why? Is there a racist in our school? A neo-Nazi? Is it serious, or just somebody trying to pull our chains? Is a student behind it, or did some adult sneak into our school with a can of red spray paint?

"I heard it was Michael Amorosa," Pamela Bynes is saying not far away from me. "Mr. Kennedy caught him in the act."

"That's crazy," Jordie Duros scoffs. "Why would *Michael* paint a swastika?"

"He didn't," Goren Lund replies. "He's just the guy who found it. He got so freaked out he dropped his phone and it broke."

"Maybe it was Mr. Kennedy," Pamela suggests. "He's always in the school."

"Mr. Kennedy's worked here forever," Jordie points out. "If he was a Nazi, we'd know by now."

Notice how I rattle off all their names. I doubt that many people in this school know Andrew and me. We're the scientists' kids. I've heard us called egglets—children of the eggheads. It's not an insult—or at least I don't think the locals mean it to be. It's just the way things are around here. It's a reminder that race and religion aren't the only things that can make you an outsider.

Andrew stays with me all the way to my homeroom, like I'm made of delicate crystal or something. I always thought he wasn't as sensitive as I am to our outsider status, but I might be wrong about that. Or maybe I look worse than I realize.

"Don't freak out," he tells me at the doorway to the class. "It's going to blow over. I promise."

"Thanks."

But when I walk into Mr. Slobodkin's homeroom, every single eye is laser-focused on me. I wonder how Andrew can make a promise like that.

If the kids are all staring at me, Mr. Slobodkin is doing the exact opposite. His effort to look anywhere else but in my direction is giving him a crick in the neck. How am I going to survive this homeroom without losing my mind?

The answer to that comes via the PA. "All classes are to meet in the auditorium in ten minutes for an important assembly."

I have a sneaking suspicion that this doesn't mean a surprise performance by a traveling troop of jugglers.

I always wondered what a sinking heart feels like. Now I know.

Our auditorium seats five hundred forty. Since there are over six hundred students in the school, the overflow has to sit on folding chairs in the orchestra pit. I'm praying for the last row of the balcony. No such luck. Mr. Slobodkin is the oldest, slowest teacher in the whole school. By the time we get down there, the only open spots are right in front of the stage. I couldn't be more on display . . . or at least that's how it feels.

In the six months since we moved to Chokecherry, I've seen Principal Brademas furious, elated, stern, excited, and even emotional. But this is a new one. He looks like he's just been dragged backward through a hedge. His face is bright red, his hair is standing on end, and his expression is more stunned than anything else. He surveys the crowd and—maybe it's just me, but—his eyes linger on the Jewish girl in the front row.

"Many of you know that our school was the target of an act of hateful vandalism last night. A white supremacist symbol was painted on the wall of our atrium. Let me stress that we know very little about this incident right now. We don't know who did it, and we don't know what that individual's motive might have been. But I felt it was important for us to get together as a school community and clear the air before the rumors get out of hand."

You'd think we're in an empty room. That's how silent it is.

"People might tell you," the principal goes on, "that the swastika on our wall is an ancient symbol, a kind of cross, that has had many meanings over the centuries. Don't believe it. Today the swastika has only one meaning: pure hatred. Most notoriously, it is the symbol of Nazi Germany, an evil regime that killed millions. It screams not just anti-Semitism, but every other kind of racism and intolerance. It is an attack against not just our minority students, but against every single one of us. And it's a hundred percent unacceptable."

A smattering of applause greets this. I don't join in. It's like my hands are made of lead.

Seated next to me, Eli Vardi offers up a high five that I just stare at.

"What's that for?" I ask him.

"Isn't this great news for you?" he demands.

"How do you figure that?"

"Brademas is anti-swastika," he explains. "And you're . . ."

I play clueless. "From Massachusetts?"

"Our custodians are in the process of removing that repulsive symbol from our atrium," Mr. Brademas goes on. "We won't have to look at it anymore, but that doesn't mean it will be gone. A swastika may be a painted picture, but it's also an idea that survives, spreading its poison long after the symbol has been erased. But there's an antidote to the poison, and that antidote is information. I'll be speaking with the school board, the teachers, and the parents. We will combat this with a tolerance education project that will involve every student and classroom. Where there's darkness, we will shine a light."

The principal kind of slumps for a moment, almost like it took everything he had to make it this far. Then he says, "I'm sorry that we have to go through this. But I hope we'll be stronger as a community when we come out the other side." And he walks off the stage, shoulders sagged.

This time the teachers applaud and maybe a few kids. Even me—I find my hands at last. But for the most part, the six hundred plus are pretty cowed. Not many of the students of Chokecherry Middle School are big Brademas fans. But when you see your principal so obviously shaken, it makes you think that maybe you should be more upset than you really are.

The next time I pass through the atrium, on the way to lunch, the wall has been repainted. You've never seen so many kids staring at a blank wall.

The swastika is gone, but it isn't.

CHAPTER FOUR

LINCOLN ROWLEY

Today's lesson is this: A swastika in your school trumps dinosaur poop in your mail slot.

Dad makes me clean up the fertilizer in the paleontology office. But here's the thing—the scientists are pretty cool about it. That kind of annoys Dad. He wanted them to threaten to call the FBI or something. This one guy, Dr. Levinson—he says his daughter goes to our school—actually admits the chicken bone is pretty funny.

The main reason I get a free pass on the dino poop is because the whole town is losing their minds over the swastika in the school. It isn't even *in* the school anymore. It took the custodians less than one assembly to wash it off and paint it over. That's part two of the lesson: Dinosaur poop is temporary; a swastika is forever.

I'm blown away. Now we're going to have a school-wide tolerance education unit because of a piece of graffiti that was on the wall for about five seconds. By the time the unit is halfway through, I'll bet no one will even remember why we started it in the first place.

Jordie, Pouncey, Sophie, and Pamela are being extra nice to me for not ratting them out over the dino poop. Except Pouncey—being nice isn't really his thing. But the others buy my lunch the next day, which is great, since it's pizza day and our cafeteria brings in from Angelino's.

"Thanks, guys," I say as we take our seats in social studies. "Some of you," I add, with a look in Pouncey's direction.

He shrugs it off. "Couldn't have killed you to shovel it up. We didn't get much fertilizer through the slot before that car came."

"Because Pam brought the wrong funnel," Jordie puts in with a grin.

Pamela kicks him under the desk.

When Mrs. Babbitt breezes into the class, the first thing she does is tape up a big sign that reads *NO PLACE FOR HATE*.

"Okay, everybody, let's get right to it. You all heard the principal, so you know what this is about. Our unit on tolerance education starts today."

"Figures," Jordie whispers. "When the elementary school wanted new playground equipment, it took three years to get it. But bring up something boring, and it's ready to go in twenty-four hours."

"I hate this," Pouncey groans.

"You can't do that here," I remind him in a low voice. "Read the sign."

Mrs. Babbitt begins by talking about World War II, the Nazi Third Reich, and the Holocaust. None of this is news to us. We all did a Holocaust unit in fifth grade at Chokecherry Elementary. But no matter how many times you study it, the numbers still grab you. In their concentration camps, the Nazis murdered eleven million people, including over six million Jews.

"Six million," the teacher repeats. "Living in a small town like ours, it's hard to imagine that many people. Even Denver's population is only a fraction of that."

We also watch a video about a middle school in a town called Whitwell, Tennessee, population 1,600. To help them make sense of a number like six million, they set out to collect six million paper clips. It seemed impossible at first, because the number was so huge and their town was so small. But word of the project spread. Paper clip donations began to pour in from all around the globe. In the end, those kids collected five times as many paper clips as they needed, and founded a world-renowned Holocaust museum.

"No wonder you can never find a paper clip when you need one," Jordie comments when the bell rings and we're heading for the door. "They're all in Tennessee."

"Never mind that," Sophie says with enthusiasm. "Those kids are celebrities! People wrote books about the paper clips project. They made a movie."

This girl Dana—one of the egglets—regards Sophie in amazement. "That's all you got out of this? That a bunch of kids ended up famous?"

None of us know the Wexford-Smythe kids that well, but Dana stands out in at least one way. She's *Jewish*—in fact, she's the only Jewish student in our school. It makes sense that she'd be extra touchy about the whole swastika thing.

"Of course not," Sophie says, embarrassed. "I just think it's cool that . . ." Her voice trails off. "I guess none of it's very cool."

Dana nods her agreement and steps out into the hall . . . but not before she shoots me a stink eye.

Pouncey sees it. "Dude, that girl hates you. Guess the magic is over."

"Or it's not effective on egglets," Jordie puts in.

I sigh. "Shut up, you guys." I understand what they're saying, though. I'm actually kind of happening at our school. A lot of that comes from being good at sports, but it hasn't really hurt me that I'm sidelined this semester. The dirty look I got from Dana—that doesn't happen very often.

That's when I remember Dr. Levinson, whose daughter goes to school here. He called her Dana. "It's the dinosaur poop," I conclude. "Her dad must have told her about it."

"She's going to flunk tolerance education," Jordie predicts. "She's already having trouble tolerating you."

We all laugh. Even Pouncey cracks a half smile.

Come to think of it, Pouncey is probably going to get an A-plus at this unit. Just living with his family, he has to do more tolerating than the rest of us put together.

Dad isn't a fan of the new tolerance education unit—but not for the same reason as the kids at school.

"No place for hate," he complains at dinner that night.

"Like we have to remind ourselves not to be terrible people! The optics couldn't be worse. And all for one little blip on our radar screen—some dumb kid who drew a swastika. Probably didn't even know what it meant."

"That's why you need tolerance education," my mother insists. "So the next dumb kid *knows* what it means and doesn't do it."

Dad gestures impatiently with his fork. "You're both missing the point. You don't call attention to one little hiccup. You wait for it to blow over. Turning it into a big deal makes the whole town look bad!"

It's like he sees his dreams of Dino-land slipping away from him. I can relate. I had dreams too—of playing soccer this fall. Remember that? Yeah, Dad, stuff happens.

Normally when Dad goes off on a rant, Mom just lets him talk. But for some reason, this swastika thing has got her on edge. I'll never forget the look on her face the night we drove to the school and saw the wall of the atrium. She didn't say a word, but she couldn't take her eyes off it, almost like she was hypnotized.

"If you ask me, showing that we take this seriously makes the town look *good*," she retorts.

Dad shakes his head. "You don't understand. The dinosaur dig is a once-in-a-lifetime opportunity. There's no limit to how much prosperity it could bring in. Kids love dinosaurs, and kids bring parents with their tourist dollars. Chokecherry could be to dinosaurs what Nashville is to country music; what New York is to theater; what LA is to movies—"

I finish his old song. "The next Orlando."

"Exactly! But when investors look for a place to put their money, they don't want to hear words like *racism* and *swastika*. They want a quiet, picture-book town in a gorgeous mountain setting, where nothing bad ever happens."

Mom raises both eyebrows halfway to her hairline. "Really, George? *Ever?*"

My father turns red as a tomato. "That was a long time ago," he mumbles. "It probably never even happened."

This is starting to get interesting. "Wait, what? What probably never happened a long time ago?"

Dad glares at my mother. "You see? This is how it starts. A few baseless rumors get around, and pretty soon you can kiss Dino-land goodbye!"

Mom looks at me. "I don't want to upset you, Link, but forty years ago, things were different around here—"

"Nicole!" Dad interrupts. "Don't tell him a crazy story like that. He'll tell his friends, and pretty soon it'll be the talk of the town!"

I'm totally hooked now. "What happened forty years ago?"

"The Ku Klux Klan," she explains. "They were here in Shadbush County."

My father regards me pleadingly. "Listen, Link. It was almost half a century ago. The world was a different place. Your mother and I weren't even born. A lot of areas had groups like that. Is it something to be proud of? Of course not. But it also isn't a reason to sacrifice everything. The Wexford-Smythe dig is an opportunity for us, but the window won't stay open forever. If we scare away our whole future dithering over a little bit of paint on a wall or some ancient history, we'll deserve what we get. Which will be nothing."

Wow. No wonder that swastika was such a big deal for the adults around here. It must have felt like the past was coming back to haunt them.

It's crazy what a few lines of paint can do: I knew it would threaten the future for Dad, but I had no idea it would dredge up a long-forgotten past for the town.

CHAPTER FIVE

MICHAEL AMOROSA

Everybody thinks I might be the one who did the swastika just because I was the first person who saw it.

That's how they talk about it too. It's never who *painted* it or who *drew* it; it's always who *did* it.

"Look at me." I plead my case across the cafeteria table. "I'm Dominican. Why would I put a racist symbol on the school? People draw racist symbols to attack *me*!"

"Seriously?" Dana Levinson leans in from her spot three chairs down. "That happened?"

"I mean in theory," I explain. "I've never experienced it in an in-your-face, swastika way. But for all we know, it was meant for me."

"Or me," adds Andrew Yee, who's having lunch with Dana. Caroline McNutt is mystified. "You guys aren't Jewish."

I roll my eyes. "They've been drilling it into our heads that a swastika isn't just anti-Jewish, it's anti-everybody— including a lot of white people who don't live or think the same way as the white supremacists."

"I just want this to be over," Dana puts in wearily. "It started because we saw a swastika for about three minutes. And now what do we do all day every day? We look at swastikas."

She has a point. Thanks to the tolerance education unit, we've seen pictures of swastikas on flags, on walls, on hats, on cars, on banners, on armbands, and on book covers. We've been shown film footage of Hitler's Third Reich and rallies by vicious hate groups and white supremacists. We've pored over the images in our textbooks and in handouts. We've even photo-shopped them into our Chromebooks, iPads, and PowerPoint presentations. I absentmindedly doodled one on my homework last night and had to tear it into a billion pieces and flush them down the toilet. That was fun—redoing my report at two in the morning just so nobody would think I'm the swastika guy. The theme may be "No Place for Hate," but if there was anybody in our school who didn't recognize the symbol on our atrium before, they sure as anything recognize it now.

"But you agree that it's important, right?" I ask her. "We can't just ignore what happened."

She thinks it over. "I guess the only thing worse than doing all this would be doing nothing."

"But it's time to move on," puts in Caroline, the seventh-grade president. "I mean, tolerance is important, but we've been doing it for almost two weeks. We're way behind in planning the Halloween dance."

I frown. "We have a Halloween dance?" I don't remember one from last year.

"We *should*," Caroline insists. "Normal schools do. Everybody always waits for the eighth-grade president to do everything. But our eighth graders are *lazy*. No offense." She glances at eighth-grade Andrew.

"Hey, I'm from Massachusetts," Andrew replies with a shrug. "This is only my school while the dig goes on. The minute my mom runs out of dinosaur bones to catalog, I'm history."

"That's a terrible attitude," Caroline scolds. "By the time the dig's over, you'll be in high school. You'll be stressing over SATs and ACTs and college admissions. Middle school should be the best years of our lives. And we're wasting them obsessing over something almost all of us didn't do that will probably never happen again."

Caroline and I have sort of a history, me being president of the art club. Whenever Caroline has a brilliant idea, she always comes to me for posters to advertise it. Last December, my team and I did thirty-six posters advertising her school-wide Secret Santa— enough to put three in every hall in the building. We really knocked it out of the park. Thanks to the awesome job we did, every kid in Chokecherry knew about it. Guess who didn't know about it—Principal Brademas. And when he put the kibosh on the whole thing, *we* were the ones who got yelled at, not Caroline. We were about three inches from having the whole art club shut down. I'm not sure what scares me more—the swastika in our atrium or the Halloween dance Caroline might make us all have.

As the tolerance education unit rolls into its third week, the only lesson anybody is learning is that you don't have to be a racist to be sick of tolerance education. I think we minority students are more sick of it than anybody, since all the kids assume we want it, which we don't. Each morning, when Mr. Brademas announces a new project we're going to do, a new lecture we're going to listen to, or a new film we're going to screen, the groan coming from every classroom in the building is enough to rattle the windows. Nobody's rude—there are no curses or catcalls or anything. We're just done. Our tolerance for tolerance education has reached its limit.

Eventually, even the teachers get the message. I know something's up when Brademas calls me to the office during my lunch period on Friday. He wants the art club to do a mural-size poster for the wall outside the office commemorating these past three weeks.

"Not the first part," the principal says quickly. "You know, what started it all. Just a few of the highlights of the tolerance education unit."

I can't resist. "Does that mean the unit is over?"

"Yes," he replies. "Please keep it to yourself. I'll make the announcement at the assembly this afternoon."

"Oh, sure," I promise, and immediately go out and spread it all over the school. Being president of the art club doesn't carry a lot of cred, so when I've got some inside scoop, I'm going to wake the town and tell the people. This could be the only chance I'll ever get to approach kids who are too cool to talk to the president of the art club—even eighth graders and popular girls like Sophie Tavener and Pamela Bynes.

Naturally, I tell everyone to keep a lid on it. And just as naturally, they find the nearest person and blab. I'll bet it doesn't take forty-five minutes before the big news reaches every ear. There's an air of electricity as we all file into the gym to hear what we already know.

It's probably a good thing that I spilled the beans before-hand, because we're pretty quiet and respectful when the principal makes the announcement. If it hadn't been for me and my big mouth, we might all have jumped up and cheered. That could have convinced Brademas that we need more tolerance education.

"I want to thank each and every one of you for the maturity and dedication that you've shown over the past three weeks," the principal concludes. "It was an unpleasant thing that brought us to this place, but I believe we're better people for it. We may never know who drew that ugly symbol, and what their purpose might have been: a sick joke, vandalism against the school, or something more sinister. But whatever the reason, it's in the past, and we can all be happy about that."

Something more sinister. I let the words sink in. They seem to say that, as one of only a handful of minority kids, maybe I should have been more freaked out than I actually was.

"And now," Mr. Brademas continues, "on to happier matters. It's time to congratulate our baseball team on their championship season this past spring."

That's the reason this assembly is taking place in the gym instead of the auditorium. It's time to unfurl the banner honoring the Chokecherry Cheetahs. It's kind of a sore point with me. Brademas uses the art club as unpaid labor for every poster and sign that goes up in the school. But when one of his precious sports teams accomplishes something, he has the banner made professionally, rolled up, and revealed in dramatic fashion in front of six hundred cheering kids.

I console myself with the thought that it's probably not going to happen again for a while. Our star athlete, Link Rowley, has been yanked out of sports because his father got steamed up over some prank gone wrong. I can't even remember which one—with Link and his pals, it's always something. So we're probably going to stay banner-free through soccer season and potentially basketball too.

The percussionist from the orchestra launches into a drumroll. At the top of a tall ladder, Mr. Kennedy loosens the twine, and the banner unfurls down the wall. The band launches into the first few notes of our fight song and falls silent. That matches the strangled gasps from the six hundred students.

The banner reads: SOUTHWESTERN COLORADO MIDDLE SCHOOL BASEBALL LEAGUE CHAMPIONS. But that's not what anybody sees. Covering the length and breadth of the fabric is a stark swastika painted in splotchy black gunk.

This time, there's none of the excitement that greeted the first swastika in the atrium. No phones appear to capture the moment in pictures and selfies. We've all been through three weeks of tolerance education, so we know exactly what we're looking at.

Something to be afraid of.

CHAPTER SIX

JORDIE DUROS

My dad's company, Duros Construction, does roofing and roof repair all around Chokecherry and Shadbush County.

Thanks a lot, Dad.

The thing is, Swastika 2.0—the one on the baseball banner—is painted in roofing tar. So the cops come to our house and search the adjoining office and warehouse. Guess what they find—roofing tar. Gallons of the stuff.

Dad's a smart aleck about it. "What do you want me to put on a roof? Bubble gum? Cole slaw?"

Cops have no sense of humor about that kind of joke. "Your boy's a seventh grader, isn't he?" Sheriff Ocasek muses with a squint eye in my direction.

Dad sticks up for me. "What's that supposed to mean?"

The sheriff shrugs. "Access to the tar. Access to the school. You do the math."

Anyway, they leave eventually. But I don't like the way they're looking at me. A lot of people in town are looking at me the same way. Or maybe I'm just being paranoid. Having your place searched by police does that to a guy.

It doesn't help that our local paper, the *Shadbush County Daily*, does a whole spread on the swastika thing.

SECOND RACIST SYMBOL RAISES MEMORIES
OF TOWN'S DARK PAST

School officials in Chokecherry were dismayed to find a second swastika painted on middle school property, this one on a banner celebrating the baseball team. This proves that the first incident three weeks ago was far from a random occurrence. The Shadbush County Sheriff's office is investigating, but still has no clear picture as to who might be behind the racist, anti-Semitic acts.

Much of the ethnic diversity in Chokecherry comes from visiting paleontologists involved in the dinosaur excavation sponsored by Wexford-Smythe University. However, there is no evidence as yet to suggest that the scientists and their families are the targets of the vandalism, although several of their children do attend the middle school.

"We're not there yet, but we'll find this guy," Sheriff Bennett Ocasek promised at a news conference at Chokecherry city hall. "Nobody should be allowed to get away with this kind of thing."

"Nothing like this has ever happened in our town before," added George Rowley, owner of Chokecherry Real Estate and president of the local chamber of commerce.

That statement is not strictly accurate. As recently as the 1970s, Shadbush County was home to an active chapter of the Ku Klux Klan. Longtime residents have not forgotten 1978's infamous Night of a Thousand Flames, when KKK groups from all over the West gathered in the county and ringed the foothills around Chokecherry with burning crosses . . .

Luckily, the article doesn't say anything about roofing tar or Duros Construction. But it gives me a bad feeling.

"You should read this," I tell Link. "They quote your dad."

The three of us are walking to school on Monday morning. That's where the paper comes from. We pass this news box every day, and Pouncey knows just where to kick it for the lid to open and give us a freebie. We usually look for our names on the local school sport report, but this swastika business is getting bigger than everything right now.

"Read it?" Link echoes bitterly. "My dad screamed the house down over it this weekend. He's afraid that any bad press for the town is going to ruin his chances of getting that dino park he's got his heart set on and turning Chokecherry into the next Orlando."

"Maybe it's payback," I suggest. "He took away your soccer season, and the price turns out to be one dino park." My thoughts turn more serious. My eyes drift across the foothills that circle the town, and I try to picture being surrounded by burning crosses in the darkness. "That Night of a Thousand Flames thing. Doesn't sound like the Chokecherry I know."

"My father says it's 'hogwash,'" Link puts in. "Is that even a word?"

"I know, right?" I high-five him. "Chokecherry's too boring for a big thing—even a *bad* big thing."

"Fake news," Link adds. "The *Daily* is so thrilled to finally have something to write about that they're losing their minds."

"My dad was there," Pouncey says from out of nowhere, gazing off into the distance.

"Your dad was *where*?" I ask him.

"The Night of a Thousand Flames," he replies in a quiet voice.

"In *1978*?" Link demands.

"He was five," Pouncey explains. "My grandfather brought him. You know how my dad's a jerk? Well, *his* dad was an even bigger one. He was in the Klan. He was in worse things than that. I guess a ring of burning crosses was his version of taking your kid out fishing."

Link holds his head. "Do me a favor: Never tell that story at my house. I've never seen my old man so uptight. And you know the worst part? My mom's worse. She freaked when she heard about the second swastika, and she doesn't give a hoot about Dino-land. She's the one who begged my dad not to invest all our savings buying up property where he thinks the resorts and golf courses are going to be."

I remember when Pouncey's grandfather died a few years ago. Not a lot of people went to the funeral. Maybe that's why—everybody remembered the KKK connection. I was clueless—I was just a little kid, there to support my friend. But it's creepy to think back, now that I know what the old man was involved in.

"But your dad's not in the Klan, right?" I ask.

Pouncey shrugs. "I don't lose too much sleep thinking about my family. Bad enough I have to live with them. But I don't think the Klan operates around here anymore. All that was back in the seventies and before."

As we step onto school property, Link brings up something I hadn't considered. "You know the worst part of this? I bet tolerance education isn't over anymore. It's going to be like *Groundhog Day*, where every morning it starts over again."

"I can't stop thinking about those six million paper clips at that school in Tennessee," I say. "I had a dream that was us and somebody drove up with one of those giant crane magnets from the car wrecking yards."

Pouncey snorts. "Maybe collecting thirty million paper clips was the only way for those guys to get their teachers to stop tolerance education."

The bell is only ten minutes away, so the lawn is crowded with kids. I wonder if any of them heard about the roofing tar, so they think I might be Swastika Guy. I see a lot of eyes on us, but that's normal. All the girls look at Link, since he's kind of the star athlete in town, and I'm not too shabby myself. But then I spot Dana Levinson's gaze on me, and there's nothing admiring about it. It's no coincidence that the girl with the most reason to be anti-swastika is staring at someone who's a prime suspect for being Swastika Guy.

"What did I do?" I blurt in her face, and she rushes away.

At the corner of the building, four Twister mats have been pegged into the grass, and about a dozen kids are wrapped around each other, pretzel-style. Caroline McNutt holds the spinner and seems to be running the game.

"Left foot—green!"

There's some shifting around, a lot of giggles, and some screams as two players bump heads. A sixth grader tumbles to the mat and has to join the spectators on the grass.

"What's going on?" Link asks.

"Get in the game!" Caroline invites. "Link's joining!" she exclaims far too loudly.

Link hangs back. "No, I'm not."

"What gives, Caroline?" I ask. "Why is it so important to give people a chance to throw up their breakfast?"

She goes on the defensive. "*Normal* schools do fun things. We've been such a bunch of sad sacks lately. It's my job as seventh-grade president to brighten things up a little."

"Considering what's been happening around here," Link points out, "maybe people aren't in a Twister mood."

"That's the whole point," she explains. "If we give in and get depressed, then the swastikas win. This is how we fight back."

"With Twister?" I ask.

"By living our lives!" she rants. "By showing whoever's doing this that a few ugly symbols aren't going to change the people we are!"

"It'll take more than swastikas to make me play Twister," Pouncey puts in.

"Oh, come on!" Caroline grabs him by the sleeve and tries to haul him onto the game, but she doesn't make much progress. Stronger people than Caroline have tried to move Pouncey. He's weighted on the bottom, like a punching clown.

The roar of a big engine captures everyone's attention. Around the corner of the building, a big delivery truck starts up and pulls away from the school's receiving dock. As it turns onto the driveway, we can now see the dumpster that stands next to the loading bay. It's there, painted in dazzling white on the dark metal bin.

Swastika number three.

CHAPTER SEVEN

LINCOLN ROWLEY

Big news from the dinosaur dig: They found a Camptosaurus skull fragment about the size of a paint chip. The scientists are pretty amped up about it, but not half as amped up as my father.

"This is exactly what we needed!" he crows. "A huge chunk of good news to take all that swastika nonsense off the front pages!"

"I wouldn't use the word *nonsense*," Mom calls over the electric motor of the treadmill in the den. She's been on a fitness kick lately—I think it helps her keep her mind off the problems at the school.

"You'll see!" Dad exclaims. "Now that the dig has produced something exciting, the publicity is going to start pouring out of here. It's happening just the way I pictured it." He sits down at the computer and opens a Google search.

I'm relieved. Dad's already warned me about how sorry I'll be if Wexford-Smythe University pulls out of here because they don't like having fertilizer dumped in their mail slot. In his eyes, the peat moss prank put my future in jeopardy. But there's nothing like a brand-spanking-new hundred-million-year-old paint chip to keep a guy's future on track.

Dad's brow furrows and the pounding of his fingers on the keyboard becomes downright violent. "What's the matter with these people? Where's my skull fragment?"

I hear Mom speeding up on the treadmill in the den.

I peer over Dad's shoulder at the screen. The search for keywords *Camptosaurus skull* brings up websites advertising *Realistic dinosaur interaction* and *Model Camptosaurus skeleton, ages 7 and up (swallowing hazard)*. When he adds *Wexford-Smythe University*, we get pictures of a tree-lined campus and the course syllabus for their infrared astronomy program.

"Try *Chokecherry*," I suggest.

I wish I hadn't. When he types the name of our town into the search field, a single word jumps out at us, appearing seventeen times on the page: *Swastika*.

Third Swastika Appears at Chokecherry Middle School . . . Swastika Graffiti Rattles Mountain Community . . . Sheriff Baffled by Swastika Incidents . . . Swastikas Dredge Up County's Racist Past.

It goes on and on.

"No wonder everybody hates the media," Dad complains bitterly. "Leave it to them to focus on the negative and ignore a major scientific find!"

I can't see Mom on the treadmill, but she must be running pretty fast. Her footsteps are rat-tat-tatting like a machine gun.

I point to one of the results in the middle of the screen. "Wow, ReelTok. He's one of the top vloggers on the web!"

Dad's brow furrows. "Vloggers?"

"Video-bloggers," I translate. "Everybody follows ReelTok."

He glares at me as if I've done something evil. "Really? You've heard of this guy?" He clicks on the link.

A YouTube clip opens up, and there's the famous face of Adam Tok, the internet personality who calls himself ReelTok. As always, he's so close to the camera that the frame shows him only from eyebrows to mid-chin. It makes him seem even more intense than he already is, with his burning eyes, rapid-fire clipped speech, and slight lisp.

"I read your comments, TokNation. Get out of the city, you tell me. Get away from the crime and the garbage and the fights to the death over a lousy parking space. Find a small town with fresh air and friendly people, where the night jasmine wafts like perfume in through your windows. Wonderful idea!" Suddenly, his unibrow arches into a V and his cheeks flame red. *How about Chokecherry, Colorado, where they paint* swastikas *at the middle school?*"

Dad hits the escape key, and ReelTok disappears. "What's with this clown, Link? It says he's from New York City. What's it his business what goes on around here?"

"That's ReelTok's trademark," I try to explain. "He starts off speaking reasonably about something and pretty soon he blows his stack and starts yelling. It's hilarious."

"But why is he yelling about Chokecherry?" Dad demands.

"It's nothing personal. He can freak out over anything. You should have seen the episode he did when his Wi-Fi went out. He blamed it on God."

My father is furious. "If you find this hilarious, then you

deserve the kind of future you're going to get. This man has never been to Chokecherry. He knows nothing about our community. But it's just fine for him to slander us to millions of people on the internet."

"He's *joking*," I insist. "Today it's Chokecherry. Tomorrow it'll be something else. The weather. Gas prices. Chocolate milk that isn't chocolaty enough."

Dad is adamant. "The chamber of commerce should sue. I'm going to put it to a vote. No one has the right to lie about our town."

"Technically, he didn't lie," I point out. "The swastikas at our school are one hundred percent real."

Dad brings down the cover of the laptop so hard it's a miracle there aren't computer keys bouncing off the ceiling. "I'm going for a walk!" he rasps, and is out of the house in a flash, slamming the door behind him.

In the silence, I notice that the treadmill isn't going anymore.

"Short workout today," I observe to Mom.

But when I poke my head into the den, I see her slumped on the loveseat looking like she's lost her last friend.

"What's the matter?" A terrible thought occurs to me. "Did Dad invest *all* our money in Dino-land?"

She's surprised. "No, nothing like that. We're fine. We just wouldn't be filthy rich, which is okay with me."

"So what's bugging you? I know Dad flips out when there's swastika news, but he always calms down in the end."

"Swastika news," she repeats wanly. "I never thought 'swastika news' was something we'd have to worry about in our lives."

"We *don't*," I insist. "I get that swastikas are dangerous when Nazis and white supremacists use them. But this is probably just some rotten kid."

"Maybe," Mom says dubiously. "But I don't like these stories about the seventies and burning crosses. If that's coming back—"

"It *isn't*," I promise. "And even if it *was*—I mean, it's not right and all that. But it wouldn't be a threat to *our* family."

To my amazement, two big tears squeeze out of her eyes and roll down her cheeks. I'm blown away. I've never seen her cry before.

"Are you okay?" I ask.

She answers with another question. "Have you ever noticed about my relatives . . . how all my cousins are on Grandpa's side and not Grandma's?"

I don't know what I expected her to say, but that wasn't it. "I never thought about it," I admit. "But it makes sense. Grandma grew up in an orphanage, right?"

She nods. "Right. In France. Did you ever consider what that might mean?"

I'm mystified. "That we're part French?"

That brings on a watery smile. "I suppose we are. But that's not the point. Grandma never knew her parents, but she wasn't orphaned at birth. Her parents gave their baby to the nuns to save her life."

"What?" This is a part of the story I haven't heard before. "Why?"

"It was 1941," Mom explains. "France was under Nazi occupation. My grandparents gave up their baby girl because they were about to be arrested and sent to a concentration camp."

"A concentration camp?" I echo in shock. "What did they do wrong?"

"Don't you get it?" she demands, fighting back more tears. "My family is *Jewish*. The nuns raised Grandma as a Catholic child, but she's Jewish too."

This isn't making any sense to me. "No, she isn't! We were there last Christmas! They had a tree and everything!"

"She never knew," Mom tells me. "Not until three years ago, when the convent released its records. She was the only survivor in my family. Her parents and all her relatives died in the Holocaust, murdered by the Nazis. By the time she found out, she had lived almost eighty years as a Christian woman. She'd married and raised her family in the faith. That's how I was brought up. But I know what my background is—and now you know yours."

I'm stunned. "We're *Jewish*?"

"Well, your dad's not. And I'm only half, which I guess makes you a quarter." She puts a reassuring hand on my shoulder. "Nothing's different, Link. We're still the same people. It'll still be Christmas and Easter. We're not changing churches or religions at this stage of the game. But when you say swastikas have nothing to do with us, that's just not true."

"Does Dad know?"

She smiles. "Of course he does. He's very supportive. That's why he's been so upset over these swastikas. I know you think he only cares about Dino-land, but it's mostly because of me. And *you*."

It's like the house is spinning all around me. How is it possible to wake up one person and, by the end of the day, you're somebody else? Jewish? Not that there's anything wrong with it, but it's a thing I'm just *not*. I don't even know anybody Jewish.

Well, not technically true. I know Dana—barely. She's not from Chokecherry, but besides that, she's pretty normal. And her dad can take a joke about dino poop, even when the joke is on him.

Finding out you're different from what you thought you were is weird. But when the difference is basically nothing, how different are you? Not at all. Right?

Right?

"When were you planning on telling me this?" I ask. "Never?"

"You're upset."

"Of course I'm upset!" I explode. "All these years I've been somebody I didn't even know I was! You're supposed to tell me big things like this!"

She looks unhappy. "I'm sorry. I was waiting for the right time, and I guess it never came. Remember, I went through this myself three years ago, so I know how confused you must feel. But I eventually understood that I'm the same me. It's an important thing to know about our past. But our present is what really matters. Our lives, our family—you, me, and Dad. That hasn't changed at all."

I back away. "You still should have told me." Mom's tearing

up again, and I'm not in the mood to feel bad about it. For the past three weeks, we've done nothing but learn about intolerance and racism and Nazism and the Holocaust, and she never said one little peep about this. I think I have the right to be mad.

Dad too—he hasn't shut up about the swastikas for five seconds since all this started. Didn't it occur to him to mention that our family might have a special interest in it? That's kind of a key piece of information, if you ask me. But nobody asks me anything.

So what now? According to Mom, I should just ignore the whole thing. But how's that supposed to work? I picture the conversation with Jordie:

Me: What were you up to today?
Jordie: Played a little ball. Helped out my old man in the shop. You?
Me: Nothing much. I found out I've been the wrong religion my whole life. Wanna play some Xbox?

Or a text exchange with Pouncey:

Pouncey: *How ru?*
Me: *Jewish*

I'm not really serious, but it suddenly hits me—Pouncey's grandfather was in the KKK. And Pouncey's dad is a notorious jerk about practically everything . . . and that includes being racist. I've never heard Mr. Pouncey say anything against Jewish people, but that's only because he doesn't know any Jewish people.

Correction: He doesn't think he does. *I'm* Jewish. Part Jewish. Twenty-five percent.

True, that doesn't mean anything about Pouncey himself. But it's kind of uncomfortable.

It wasn't uncomfortable yesterday, even though I understood how awful the Klan was. What's different? Yesterday I didn't *know*.

So much for Mom's idea that nothing has changed. Another lie.

To be fair, my parents didn't technically *lie*. But only because it never occurred to me to ask them, "Say, we wouldn't happen to be Jewish, would we?"

Mom thinks this is no biggie. She got used to it; why can't I? It'll fade into the background as soon as my life gets busy again, with friends, sports, school—

At the thought of the school, I get a clear vision of the big red swastika, freshly painted in the atrium. It's the same symbol, same color, same right angles. But I can feel the hair on the back of my neck standing up at the sight of it. I picture Grandma, as a little baby, being handed over to total strangers. And never seeing her family again.

My mind runs through everything we learned about Nazi Germany these past three weeks of tolerance education, and during the Holocaust unit in fifth grade. It used to seem like *ancient* history . . . but this happened to *my* family. Where are my cousins on Grandma's side? They were never born, because their parents and grandparents were murdered by the Nazis.

I feel like I'm losing it. All these ideas are whirling around my brain, building up the pressure until my skull starts to crumble. I've got to find a way to let it out—talk to somebody maybe. But who?

My parents?

They're the ones who kept me in the dark all these years.

My friends?

They'd be just as weirded out as I am.

Is there anyone around here who'd understand?

CHAPTER EIGHT

DANA LEVINSON

I have swastika anxiety.

I see them everywhere—in clouds, in wallpaper patterns, in the weave of a rug. Once your brain goes in that direction, it'll drive you crazy. I see one in my spaghetti, and no matter how many times I push my dinner around with a fork, the noodles keep re-forming into that awful pattern.

Eventually, my little brother, Ryan, notices me staring into the bowl with a murderous look in my eyes. So he takes that as the okay to reenact the Battle of Gettysburg on his plate, complete with sound effects of gunfire and muted cries of "Charge!" Pretty soon, tomato sauce is splattering all over the table.

Dad sighs. "If you don't like it, you two, you don't have to eat it. But please stop making a mess."

This from a guy who spends his days carving fossils out of sandstone using a chisel and a paintbrush. He usually comes home looking like he's taken a mud bath—at least that's what my mother says. She works with the scientists too, cataloging their finds. So she stays clean most of the time.

The only thing worse than seeing swastikas where they're not is dreading where they'll turn up next. Whoever's doing all this must feel pretty strongly about it, because they're putting the awful things everywhere—scratched into lockers, duct-taped to windows, decorating bulletin boards and display cases.

There have been a total of eight incidents, and nobody has a clue who's doing it. The school has even hired extra security to try to catch the culprit in the act. So far no luck. They have only one theory—that the guilty party is a kid. Every day, six hundred of us show up for school, and there aren't enough employees in the district and cops in town to spy on each and every one of us.

I don't have to see it to know that a new swastika has popped up somewhere. Suddenly, people are being friendly to me and noticing I'm alive. How am I doing, they ask. How am I holding up, considering, you know. I get that they're just trying to be nice. Does it make me a bad person that I find their sympathy almost as upsetting as the swastikas that bring it on? Andrew and the other Asian kids don't get that kind of attention. And nobody worries about the Black and Latino kids, who probably don't feel great about this either. It's just me, the Jewish girl.

I can't get past the feeling that this is just some juvenile delinquent trying to freak everybody out. And the worst part is, it's working. All those stories from the seventies—burning crosses, Ku Klux Klan. What if our family becomes a target?

My parents have been checking in with me every day. I'm under strict orders to tell them if anyone says or does something threatening. They're a little more hands off with Ryan—nobody wants to traumatize a second grader. But even he gets a nightly stealth interrogation: Have you noticed friends treating you differently lately? Have you been overhearing new words you don't understand?

One day, he asks, "What's a swampika?"

Mom doesn't miss a beat, almost like she was expecting it. "It's a wet, muddy place where tadpoles and lizards live."

She says it so naturally, so matter-of-factly, that my brother accepts it and moves on. I envy my little brother. I hope he gets to stay clueless forever, but I doubt it. The swastikas are big news and getting bigger.

Dad has been driving Ryan and me to school instead of making us walk. So much for "Kids don't get enough fresh air and exercise anymore."

I watch as Ryan slams the car door and scampers into his elementary school. "I wish I was seven. Ryan's biggest worry is what flavor of pudding pop Mom packed in his lunch."

Dad doesn't take the bait, probably because he knows where I'm going with this. Sometimes, it's not that great being raised by two PhDs. They're always miles ahead of you. He steers our SUV into the road and starts across the neighborhood toward the middle school.

This time I say it outright. "Dad, do you think the university would transfer you and Mom to another town?"

He glances sideways at me. "Well, we were trying for Paris, but turns out there aren't any Diplodocus skeletons buried under the Eiffel Tower."

"It isn't exactly fun, you know," I complain, "being the only Jewish kid while all this swastika stuff is going on."

He pulls up in front of the student drop-off. "Mom and I know it can't be pleasant. We both grew up in places where we were far from the only Jewish kids . . . and we knew coming here would be an adjustment, even before these incidents began."

"Yeah, but *now*—"

"From what I've seen, your school is staying on top of it. Nobody's trying to sweep this under the rug. I believe they'll find out who's doing it. And my hope is that we'll all see that it's just thoughtless mischief and poses no danger to this family. However"—he looks me straight in the eye—"if you or your brother are unsafe in any way, we will not stay here. Period."

"But I still have to go to school," I conclude wearily.

"But you still have to go to school."

I sigh and get out of the car. Dad might be right about the true motivation behind the swastikas, but he doesn't have to be me. He doesn't know what it's like, expecting to see *it* on the office bulletin board or the atrium wall. He can't understand how it feels to scan a crowd of faces, searching for the expression of sympathy that says it's happened again. Welcome to my world.

No stares today. Could I get that lucky? I'm almost all the way down the main hall, and not a single person has pulled me aside to tell me how sorry they are about the bad news.

Uh-oh. Someone is standing in front of my locker. Wait— that's Link Rowley. He's kind of the star-athlete Big Man on Campus around here. He's also the guy who pranked my father's office. I sincerely doubt he wants anything to do with me.

"Dana, can I talk to you?"

So much for that theory. "Okay—uh, what about?"

He looks around furtively, like an escaped convict keeping an eye out for the police. "Not here."

He grabs my arm and drags me to the stairwell. He waits for a couple of kids to disappear up the steps before speaking. And even then it's a barely audible whisper.

"I can't hear you," I say self-consciously. I'm not used to popular boys talking to me in any school, much less this one. What's going on?

"I said I think I'm Jewish."

Whatever shyness I might have had around him vanishes as my anger flares. "You think that's funny after everything that's been happening?"

"No, seriously! I—"

I just about bite his head off. "How many of your idiot friends are about to jump out and have a good laugh at the Jewish girl?"

"It isn't like that at all! Listen to me!"

The story that pours out of him is too stunning to be a joke—that his grandmother was handed over as a baby to nuns to escape the Nazis. She was the only one of her Jewish family to survive the Holocaust.

"That's awful!" I tell him, and I mean it. "But why are you just bringing this up now?"

"I only found out yesterday," he explains earnestly. "Nobody ever told me. But this swastika business has got my mom all upset."

I take stock of him. He's 1,000 percent serious and pretty

emotional about it too. Unless he's the greatest actor in history, I totally believe that he's just found this out about himself.

"I can see how that's pretty heavy news," I tell him.

"I know. That's why I came straight to you."

That brings me up short. "To me? Why?"

He regards me in surprise. "Because you're Jewish."

"So?"

"So maybe you can tell me . . . you know . . . what to do."

I'm at a total loss. My great-great-grandparents emigrated to America at the turn of the twentieth century; any relatives of mine who died in the Holocaust were cousins of ancestors I never knew. Nothing nearly as close as what Link just described.

"What do your parents say?" I ask him.

"They want to ignore the whole thing," he tells me. "But you can't listen to them. They're the ones who kept me in the dark. I'm not going to let them stop me from being who I am."

"Wait a minute." I struggle for the right words. "Are you saying you want to *be* Jewish? Like, change your religion?"

He shrugs unhappily. "I don't know. It's not like religion is a big part of my life to begin with. We're not regular church-goers or anything like that."

"We're not that religious either," I tell him. "We don't keep kosher or go to services every week. We're a hundred miles from the nearest synagogue, and my family's okay with it. We still celebrate holidays, but we do it our own way. My parents are fossil hunters. Their careers are more important to them than being religious."

"But you're definitely Jewish, right?"

He seems so anxious about it that I have to laugh. "A hundred percent," I assure him. "In fact, you are too, technically. The tradition is it goes by the female line. If your grandmother's Jewish, and your mother's Jewish, then so are you."

His face grows animated. "See, that's the kind of thing I need to know! What else have you got?"

I smile. "I'm not a rabbi. Why is this so important to you?"

For someone who's never struck me as being the kind of guy who chooses his words carefully, Link seems to be thinking very hard about what he wants to say. "I can't quite explain it. All my life, it's been like everybody knows more about me than I do. My dad talks about my future as if he sees it and I don't. My friends look at me as a certain kind of person—sporty, popular, a joker. And that fits . . . but not all the way. Now suddenly I find out that I've been somebody different from the start. I'm confused about whether the things I'm doing are actually things I *should* be doing. You know?"

It's as if the shock of this news jump-started his brain . . . and I have no idea what to tell him. I'm not the official Welcoming Committee for Judaism—but I recognize I'm all he's got. And one of the things I do know about being Jewish is that we don't turn our backs on people who come to us for help.

The bell rings, offering rescue from this very unexpected conversation. "Okay," I venture, "thanks for, uh, sharing—" I start walking away.

"But we're not finished!" he protests.

"We have homeroom."

"You can't leave me hanging," he insists. "You've been Jewish your whole life, but I'm thirteen years behind. I have no idea what to do."

The number thirteen sticks in my brain.

"Bar mitzvah lessons," I blurt.

He goggles at me. He has no idea what I'm talking about.

"That's what a thirteen-year-old Jewish guy is usually doing," I explain. "Preparing for his bar mitzvah. Really—I have to go." And before he can reply, I step into the stampede of kids that fills the hallway.

When I glance over my shoulder, Link is still in the stairwell, a stunned expression on his face.

CHAPTER NINE

LINCOLN ROWLEY

Dad's eyes are as wide as saucers. "You want to be *Jewish*?"

"That's not what I'm saying," I tell him. "I'm saying I want to have a bar mitzvah."

"Which is something Jewish people have!"

"If you go by the rules, I'm as Jewish as anybody," I argue. "I get it from Mom, and she gets it from Grandma. I spoke to Dana Levinson a couple of times at school today, and she explained the whole thing. And I checked it out on Google."

My father's tone drips with sarcasm. "Well, if *Google* says it's okay, then by all means, let's turn our lives upside down and change everything about ourselves."

"You're not listening," I insist. "I don't want to change everything. I just want to try this and see how it feels. I'm thirteen, which is perfect bar mitzvah timing."

My mother has been silent for most of this conversation, trying to shrink behind the pork chop on her plate. She's pretty shaken up, but I don't think she's as determined as my father to say this isn't happening. For one thing, Dad keeps glancing in her direction, expecting her to jump in and support him. It hasn't happened. Mostly, she just looks torn.

Finally, she speaks up. "I didn't know being Jewish follows the mother's line."

"So you're Jewish too," I inform her. "You could have a bat mitzvah—Dana had hers right before she moved here. You'd be kind of late, though. Like, twenty-seven years."

"No, thank you," she replies faintly. "But, Link—this is just not practical. There's no synagogue in Chokecherry."

"I thought of that. The nearest one is in Shadbush Crossing. Temple Judea."

"That's a hundred miles away!" Dad explodes.

"Yeah, but we'll only have to go once—for the actual thing," I reason. "Rabbi Gold says—"

"Hold up!" Dad pushes his plate away, his dinner untouched. "Who's Rabbi Gold?"

"I called over there," I supply. "He's pretty chill. And Temple Judea is Reform, which is *super* chill. Their take on the rules is more welcoming for someone like me. Most of their bar and bat mitzvah kids have been learning Hebrew since they were little, so I'm way behind. But the rabbi says that if I'm really, truly committed to this, he can design a kind of bar mitzvah crash course—he'll write the Hebrew parts out phonetically so I don't have to learn a whole different alphabet. I'll practice at home and work with him on Zoom. But he wants to talk to you guys before we pick out a date. You know, just to make sure everything's kosher." I wink.

My father actually flinches, like I've taken a swipe at him. Typical. It's always about him.

"You know why the rabbi wants to talk to us, Link?" he asks. "Because he notices—as we do—that all this is complete and total nonsense!"

I've been expecting this, and I already know what I'm going to say. "It isn't really, when you think about it. I get that it's unusual. But if you take all the details one by one, nothing is nonsense. The Jewish part is totally on the up and up—even Rabbi Gold says so. Learning my bar mitzvah part phonetically is doable, especially since the rabbi is willing to work with me on Zoom. And Shadbush Crossing isn't the moon, so it won't kill us to drive there one Saturday."

Dad's unimpressed. "Just because something's doable doesn't mean you have to do it. I know you, Link. You're not feeling any great religious calling. If you've been to church a dozen times in your life, it's a lot—and even then you had to be dragged, kicking and screaming. You think it'll be any different if there's a Star of David on the hymnbook instead of a cross? What's all this really about?"

I sit back with a sigh. There's no way to explain it to him. There's no way to tell him *everything* . . . and even the parts of it I understand aren't the kind of things we ever talk about. Do I suddenly feel the need to have another religion? No. Is my life now going to be all about Judaism? No. But my life should be about *something*, even if I haven't figured out what it is yet.

A lot of things have happened lately to get me thinking about that. So when Mom told me the truth about Grandma, I couldn't just file it away under *Who Cares?* and go back to being the old me. I picture my grandmother, all four foot ten of her. We've been measured back-to-back ever since I was old enough to stand. I've been taller from the age of nine on up. How could something so huge have happened to someone so small?

I'm as honest as I can be with him. "I wish I could tell you, Dad. It's like I'm exploring, even though I don't really know what I'm looking for. The rabbi says this could be my way of honoring Grandma's relatives who died in the Holocaust, and all my cousins who never got the chance to be born. The only thing I'm sure of is I have to try."

My mother gets up, walks over to my chair, and hugs me so hard I can't breathe for a moment. "That's beautiful," she says with a little sniffle. "Especially with this horrible swastika business going on."

Dad knows when the jig is up. "All right," he grumbles. "I never thought these words would come out of my mouth, but . . . let's have a bar mitzvah."

I corner Dana in the cafeteria line the next day at lunch. "Hey, what are you doing December fourth?"

She regards me warily. "I don't know. Why?"

I beam at her. "Well, save the date, because you're invited to my bar mitzvah."

She staggers a little, and a bowl of hot vegetable soup topples off her tray and lands on my sneakers.

"Oh—sorry—" she apologizes.

I grab a fistful of napkins and dab at my shoes. "Not exactly the reaction I was expecting. I thought you'd be happy."

"This is a joke, right?"

"No, I'm serious," I tell her. "It's at Temple Judea in Shadbush Crossing. Ten a.m. Your whole family's invited, since you'll need a ride."

She looks horrified. "But I was only *kidding* about the bar mitzvah!"

"Yeah, but I wasn't. You were right about the female-line thing. Rabbi Gold says I'm a hundred percent legit."

"It's just that"—she's grasping for the right words—"when I had my bat mitzvah, I'd been in Hebrew school since I was seven. You can't just start from scratch now and be ready by December."

"Already taken care of," I assure her. "Rabbi Gold's hooking me up with everything I need written out phonetically. I won't have to learn how to read Hebrew. And he'll tell me what it all means, so we can talk about it. He's big on making sure I understand what I'm saying. Don't worry, Dana. I've got this. So what do you think?"

Her lower lip quivers. "It's all my fault!"

"Huh?"

"When I said you should be practicing for your bar mitzvah, I was just trying to get rid of you so I could go to homeroom! It was a joke! Even when you kept asking about it . . . I didn't expect you to call a rabbi! *We* don't even have a rabbi in this town!"

"Well, you might have been kidding, but you were right.

Just because you weren't serious doesn't mean it wasn't great advice. So you're a yes for December fourth?"

She's flustered. "Uh—I'll have to ask my folks."

"To be honest," I go on, "I was hoping to hit you up for a little help once Rabbi Gold emails me the stuff I have to learn. You know, since you've been through this already."

She's been holding her tray for this entire conversation, so her arms are probably getting tired, even though her lunch must be lighter without the soup.

"I should eat now," she says.

"Sure. Let's find a spot."

I follow her to one of the long tables, where she establishes herself near Andrew Yee, Michael Amorosa, and Caroline McNutt. Jordie and Pouncey are waving at me to join them at the table where they're eating with Pamela and Sophie. I wave back but set down my brown-bag lunch next to Dana. It would be a jerk move to abandon her right after hitting her up for a favor.

There's a lively conversation going on between Andrew, Michael, and Caroline, but by the time Dana and I sit down, it's all petered out and the three are staring at me. Those guys aren't really my crowd. Michael's artsy, Caroline's into student government, and Andrew's another one of the scientists' kids, like Dana.

"What's up?" I say, to break the ice.

"We're talking about the student council meeting after school," Caroline explains.

Michael delivers an elaborate fake yawn, and she snaps

at him, "Well, that's the whole problem. Nobody ever comes to council meetings because they're boring, but today's is really important. We need to come up with a response to the swastikas—something so strong that whoever's doing it will see this is not who we are, and we're not going to take it anymore." She turns to Dana. "You're coming, right?"

"We-e-ell . . ." Dana hems and haws.

Caroline cuts her off. "You have to be there. You're the only Jewish kid in the whole school."

"Not true," I burst in.

Caroline frowns. "Who else is there?"

"Me." There's stunned silence around the table, so I go on. "Okay, it's pretty new, but it's definitely true. I just found out, so I'm taking it slow. Step one is my bar mitzvah. Dana's idea."

Dana sinks a little lower in her seat.

Caroline is the first to recover her voice. "So you're coming too, right?"

Fact: I would rather be deep-fried in boiling oil than sit through one of Caroline's student council meetings. But once again, the image of that first swastika comes back to me, and I feel a chill down my spine. I understand it better now. It's hard for me to imagine Grandma's family dying in the Holocaust, since for sure they'd all be gone by now anyway. It's Rabbi Gold who planted the phantom cousins in my mind—the ones who never had a chance to be born. One student council meeting is a small price to pay for all of them.

"We'll be there," I promise Caroline.

CHAPTER TEN

CAROLINE MCNUTT

"The meeting is in the library at three thirty sharp," I tell the kids waiting in line at the used-tray return in the cafeteria. "You don't want to miss it."

"I don't know." Tabitha Willebrand makes a face. "I've got plans at four. Some friends are going to the mall."

"Bring them along," I urge. "We need everybody's ideas. We're going to decide on what to do about the swastikas once and for all." When she doesn't answer, I add, "Link's going to be there."

"No way," she says flatly. "Link Rowley? At a student council meeting?"

"He personally promised me."

And she upgrades her RSVP to a maybe.

I always knew that we could get more people excited about student government if the popular kids were more into it. Link probably means Jordie, since they're the top jocks. Jordie probably means Pamela, since they've been basically engaged since Gymboree. It's like dominos. Once they start knocking each other down, who knows where it's going to end?

I'm a little conflicted, since I'm against the idea of everybody worshipping the so-called cool crowd. But if Link's name can bring a decent turnout to this very important meeting, then it's worth it.

I try again in the second-floor bathroom with the small group of girls hanging around the sinks. "Don't forget the student council meeting after school. Link wants everybody to be there."

And later at the drinking fountain. "Three thirty in the library. Student council meeting. Don't let Link down."

Sophie chokes over a mouthful. "You're bugging. No way Link's going to that."

"Oh yes he is. He told me at lunch."

Sophie doesn't look convinced. On the other hand, she has not just a Link connection, but a Jordie connection and a Pamela connection too. I'd bet money that she's already wondering why Link ate lunch with us today instead of with her and Pamela. If *Sophie* spreads the word, we might need a bigger room. Either way, it's bound to be better than our last meeting, where not a single person showed up except me—and that includes the other council members.

Sure enough, when I make my way to the library after last period, the chairs are filled and there are even a few standees at the back. It isn't the vast mob scene I'd been hoping for, but there must be forty kids, maybe fifty. I get a little teary-eyed at the sight of them. This is what school government is about—students uniting to take on a tough problem that affects all of us. Okay, I understand that most of them only came because of the rumors I started about Link. The important thing is they're here, so I've got them.

Only . . . I scan the room . . . where is Link? I see Dana sitting next to Michael and Andrew. Tabitha came. So did Sophie, who's with Jordie, Pamela, and Clayton Pouncey. They're standing next to the door, probably so they can make their escape if the meeting isn't exciting enough. Come to think of it, a lot of the attendees are peering expectantly into the hall. If Link doesn't show, I have a feeling I'm going to be alone again. I consider asking Mr. Brademas to lock the library doors from the outside, but that might violate the fire code. Bummer.

Daniel Faraz, the eighth-grade president, leans over to me. "What's the deal, Caroline? You said Link's going to be here."

I'm panicking now. "I never told you that."

"Well, no. But you told Tabitha, who told Jeffrey, and he snapchatted Lucas, who told me."

I'm sweating big-time. I have no answer. But at that moment, Link strolls in, the school hero, fashionably late. There's an audible sigh of relief in the room, most of it from me.

Mr. Brademas quiets everybody down and signals Daniel to start the meeting. Technically, he's top banana as president of the eighth grade, even though he only ran for office to impress Suzy Kraft, who dumped him anyway, the day after the election.

We start off with this whole debate about whether or not the minibus that takes the mathletes to the big tournament in Denver has Wi-Fi or not. I feel like my head is going to explode. Somebody is drawing symbols of racial hatred all over the school, and we're talking about Wi-Fi? I can see kids' eyes glazing over; Sophie and her crew are inching toward the door. Oh no! I'm going to lose this crowd I worked so hard to gather.

I leap to my feet. "I move that the Wi-Fi question should be brought up at the next meeting. Anybody opposed? No? Motion passed!"

Everybody claps. I wasn't expecting it, but I'll take it. Daniel sits down, looking like he's accomplished something.

Finally, it's my turn. I had a long speech planned, but at the last second, I junk it. Nobody loves political theater more than me. But something really awful has been going on, and the best approach is just to be honest.

"Let's talk about the swastikas. Yeah, I know everybody's against them, but they keep coming." I turn to the principal. "And, no offense, Mr. Brademas, but tolerance education isn't working, and we can't do it forever anyway. We have to try something new."

I look out over the crowd. No one is leaving now. Kids seem interested and serious. Heads are nodding in agreement, and at least a dozen hands go up. I call on people to have their say—and it isn't just Dana and Michael and Andrew, and the other minority students who have the most reason to feel threatened.

"You hear about this kind of thing happening in other places, but I never thought it would come to Chokecherry."

"It makes everyone in our town look like idiots."

"My parents are thinking about moving out of the county."

"I hate coming to school in the morning. You never know what you're going to find on what wall."

"ReelTok is telling the whole internet we're Nazis!"

A few kids think we're overreacting. Why should we change our lives because of one bad apple? For all we know, the person behind this isn't even a true racist, just a joker with a sick sense of humor. It isn't our job to stop this; we should wait for the police to catch the perpetrator.

I don't agree with everybody, but there are no jerks. All the opinions are thoughtful and sincere. I feel a surge of energy. This is democracy!

Mr. Brademas looks at his watch. "You all bring up excellent points. What we need now are suggestions—a plan of action. Where do we go from here?"

Democracy gets really quiet really fast. Even I can't think of anything to say. You can talk about a problem all day long. But coming up with a solution? That's a lot harder.

Dana speaks up. "Most of us aren't bad people inside, but obviously there's at least one. I wish it was different, but there's nothing we can do."

Coming from a girl everyone knows is Jewish, the words land hard.

"That's not good enough."

All eyes turn to Link. He's the reason most of them are even here, but this is the first time he's opened his mouth.

"It's easy for you to say," Link tells Dana. "Your folks will dig up a few more dinosaur bones and you'll be gone. The rest of us have to live here. You see how bad it gets. First it's swastikas, and soon everybody's talking about the seventies and burning crosses and the KKK. The paper clips school in Tennessee is right near where the Klan got its start, and they didn't just let it go. They did something about it."

"You think we should collect paper clips too?" Jordie asks.

"During World War II, the people of Norway wore paper clips on their clothes as a protest against the Nazis," Mr. Brademas puts in. "But in Whitwell, the point wasn't so much the paper clips as the *number*. Who can even imagine six million Jews murdered during the Holocaust? The collection was to give the students a picture of six million of anything. Each paper clip corresponded to a life exterminated for nothing, and the enormity of the collection represented the vastness of the crime against humanity."

"The paper clip idea was great," I offer. "But we shouldn't have to copy another school. Why can't we come up with our own collection—something that represents our town?"

"How about chokecherries?" Daniel suggests. "Every bush in the foothills is full of them."

Mr. Brademas steps in. "I love the symbolism, Daniel, but it isn't practical. Paper clips don't rot; berries do."

"Ever eat those things?" Pouncey puts in. "It's like a stress test for your plumbing."

An animated babble rises from the crowd. Everybody has a story to tell about the dangers of eating too many chokecherries. They aren't poison, but I can't remember ever having such miserable cramps. Let's just say that if all you do is choke on them, you're getting off easy.

"Focus, people!" I exclaim in an effort to get the group back on topic. "If we put our minds together, we can come up with the perfect thing. First, it can't be something that goes bad. Second, we need to be able to get six million of it, so it can't be too big or heavy or expensive. And third, it has to show whoever's doing the swastikas that we're all connected as a school community, and one evil person can't break us apart."

"A chain!" Michael, who's head of the art club, stands up, his face alight with excitement. "A paper chain—with six million links!"

As soon as the words are out of his mouth, I know it's right. A paper chain! Interlocking loops of multicolored construction paper—six million of them for the six million Jewish lives snuffed out during the Holocaust. But it's also a picture of unity, the interconnecting links like a long line of people standing arm in arm against intolerance and hate.

I'm not the only one who loves the idea. The crowd starts buzzing about it. It's just so *possible*. We've all been making paper chains since we were in kindergarten!

"Now wait just a minute." Mr. Brademas holds up a hand. "Let's consider the logistics. Paper clips come in boxes of hundreds or more. A paper chain has to be made one link at a time. Cut the paper, form the loop, glue it closed. Six million is an awfully big number."

"That's why this is so perfect!" Michael exclaims. "We'd be *doing* something, not just buying something. It's an even better way to experience how huge six million is."

"And it wouldn't be just *us*," I add. "The whole school would be helping."

"We only have a little over six hundred students," the principal reasons. "Even with everybody participating, that would mean each and every one of us would have to be responsible for ten thousand links of chain. It's not realistic to think we could accomplish it."

That dumps a bucket of water on the campfire, and the buzz in the room dies down a little.

It's Link, of all people, who comes to the rescue. "Maybe that's the whole point. Six million isn't supposed to be easy. Can every kid in school make ten thousand links for a paper chain? I don't know. But by trying, we're going to understand just how many people were killed during the Holocaust . . . like my grandmother's whole family."

Mr. Brademas sits forward in amazement. "Like *your* grandmother's—Surely you're not implying—Would you explain that, please, Lincoln?"

At lunch, when Link said he was Jewish, I figured he was just being dramatic about how anti-swastika he was. But the story he tells us has all our jaws hanging open. Link's grandmother is a Holocaust survivor! Even though it happened so many years ago and so far away, our school has a direct connection to the Holocaust! If that's not a sign that the paper chain project is the way to go, I don't know what is.

All eyes are on Mr. Brademas. The principal is sweating now. If he shuts this idea down after what we've just heard, he's a cockroach doing the backstroke in the iced tea pitcher.

Maybe I tricked most of the kids into coming by dropping Link's name, but he's turned out to be the star of the meeting.

When Mr. Brademas finally speaks, his words are slow and deliberate, like he's choosing them very carefully. "So long as everybody understands that we're probably not going to make it anywhere near one million, much less six, then I think it's a worthy response to the person or persons who have been defacing our building."

He probably has more to say, but everybody bursts into applause and cheers, drowning him out. At least a dozen people swarm around Link, battering him with backslaps and high fives. That's a little annoying, since it was Michael's idea, not his. Why do the popular people always get even more popular? But I have no complaints, because this was the best student council meeting I've ever had. To see a whole group of kids so excited about a school activity that they howl with joy when we get the go-ahead is a dream come true.

I get so wrapped up in the moment that I holler, "Three cheers for student government!"

It wrecks the mood. I get a lot of weird looks as people file out of the library. Even Mr. Brademas is shaking his head.

I don't care. The paper chain project is on, and that's the main thing.

CHAPTER ELEVEN

LINCOLN ROWLEY

Watching soccer practice brings me a pang that's part longing, part regret, and part resentment. How can they have the team without me? Stupid, I know. Nobody's going to cancel the season because of one kid, no matter how good he is. But it hurts to see Jordie on the field in my striker spot, doing passing drills with Erick Federov, the eighth grader who's our captain.

I feel yet another flash of anger toward Dad. It's his fault I'm on the sidelines. I have a brief vision of the semi sliding across the intersection into that pole, the showers of sparks from the damaged transformer. I wish I could say it was worth it, but it wasn't. I'm always doing stuff like that because of how funny it'll be, and it never is. You think I'd learn. The more hilarious the prank, the angrier it makes everybody, including me.

Anyway, if there ever was a sports season to miss, this is the one. I'm studying for my bar mitzvah and the paper chain is supposed to start tomorrow. So maybe this is for the best.

"Didn't expect to see you here," comes a voice from over my shoulder.

Pouncey is flat on his back across the third row of bleachers, a half-open eye on me.

"Just because I'm off the team doesn't mean I can't come to support Jordie," I tell him.

He sits up. "Yeah, but shouldn't you be moaning and groaning in some foreign language?"

I laugh. "It only sounds like moaning and groaning. It's really saying stuff. Rabbi Gold is teaching me what it means. That's important, because I have to write a speech about it."

He's horrified. "A *speech*? Man, what else do have to do? Stick flaming bamboo under your fingernails?"

"I'm also learning a lot about the history of Judaism," I admit.

"I used to know this kid named Link Rowley," Pouncey informs me. "You would have liked him. If anybody asked him to do extra school, or sing in Hebrew, or make a speech, he would have laughed in their faces. And the last thing he ever would have thought of would be to get his whole school working on a paper chain."

"Hey, you can't pin the paper chain on me," I retort. "It wasn't even my idea." That was Michael.

On the field, a whistle ends soccer practice, and Jordie heads toward us. From the track, Pamela and Sophie jog over.

"The rabbi's here," Pouncey announces with a thumb in my direction.

I feel my face flaming red. "Give me a break, you guys."

Sophie gives me a probing look. "What's the deal with you and Dana Levinson? Is she your *girlfriend* now?"

"Of course she's not my girlfriend! I don't *have* a girlfriend."

"You eat lunch with her *every day*," Pamela persists.

"So I can ask her questions," I try to explain. "She had a bat mitzvah—that's the girl version. This whole thing is so new to me. I need *help*."

"So why do it at all?" Jordie says. "Stick with us. You don't need help with what we do."

"We're basic," Pouncey puts in proudly.

"It's still me," I say stubbornly. "This thing with my grandmother hit me really hard."

"She isn't Jewish either," Jordie argues.

"Oh yeah?" I challenge. "If her parents hadn't hidden her with the nuns and the Nazis had gotten hold of her, do you think *they* would have considered her not Jewish? Even me—okay, I wasn't alive back then, but if I had been, what would have happened to a guy with my relatives? That Holocaust unit—that could have been *me*."

They're quiet for a long moment. Finally, Jordie says, "Dude." It's only one syllable, but it speaks paragraphs.

"That's why I feel like I have to try this," I tell them.

"Being Jewish," Sophie finishes, still skeptical.

"Let's just start with the bar mitzvah. I'll figure out the rest of it as it comes up. For all I know, I'll wake up on December fifth and it'll be totally out of my system."

"Just in time for Christmas," Jordie observes optimistically.

"You're not trying to double-dip, are you?" Pouncey asks suspiciously. "Like, you rake in the Hanukkah presents and then switch back on Christmas Eve."

"It isn't about presents," I insist. "I don't know what it's about. But I need to find out."

"Then we're with you all the way," Pamela assures me, and Jordie and Sophie chime in their agreement.

"Are you guys with *me* all the way?" Pouncey demands. "I'm starting my own religion and the Festival of Eating Sacred Pizza is coming up—your treat."

It breaks the mood. Everybody laughs. Leave it to Pouncey to cap off the conversation with something nuts.

But I can't help thinking back to Pamela when she told me how supported I am. The look on her face seemed to say she thought this was idiotic and she didn't support it one bit.

For all I know, none of them do.

CHAPTER TWELVE

MICHAEL AMOROSA

Me and my big mouth.

I'm the one who's always complaining about everybody using the art club as a free poster-making service. And what do I do? Sign us up for six million paper chain links.

Okay, Mr. Brademas only gave us the green light because he's positive we're not going to get anywhere near that number. Even if we had the time and the ability, we'd run out of construction paper long before we got close. There probably isn't that much construction paper in all of Colorado. Six million links might as well be infinity links.

And when we don't make it, who is everybody going to blame?

Me and my big mouth.

Actually, I think Mr. Brademas would have said no if it wasn't for the story about Link's grandmother. That blew everybody's mind, including the principal's. A whole family wiped out except for one little baby. No wonder Link wants to have a bar mitzvah. I don't know how I'd react, but I think I'd want to find a way to connect to the heritage I never knew I had—especially when fresh swastikas are popping up all around me every day. The latest is on the ice cream freezer in the cafeteria.

Everyone was more upset at not getting ice cream than they were about finding another you-know-what. Maybe we're the wrong school to take on a six-million-link paper chain. Or maybe that proves we need the paper chain project more than anybody.

So far, nobody has the faintest idea who the swastika guy—or swastika girl—might be. The police have been hanging around the school a lot, interviewing kids and keeping their eyes open. Maybe their plan is to keep the pressure on until the guilty party breaks down and confesses. I'm not holding my breath. To paint one swastika on a wall, all you have to be is a jerk. But anybody rotten enough to do fourteen of them, and to keep on doing it even though the whole town is freaking out over them? That person isn't going to lose their nerve just because there are a few cops around.

To be honest, I don't have a lot of faith in Sheriff Ocasek's investigation. For starters, I'm *still* a prime suspect, because I'm the only person who was ever caught alone with one of the swastikas.

"It's not just that," the sheriff tells me. "You're the head of the art club, right? You've got the key to that supply closet. Lots of paint in there—including spray paint."

"But—but—but—but—" Swastika Guy might be great at holding up under pressure; I'm pure mush. "Why would I do anything like that?"

"Maybe you're the kind of kid to light a spark in the barn just to watch it burn. One thing I've learned in my years in law enforcement: If you commit to any one theory of what's in a perp's head, you'll miss what's right in front of your face—that's cop talk for *perpetrator*." He hands me his business card from the Shadbush County Sheriff's Department. "Any time you feel like talking," he invites. "Oh, and your parents already have my card, just in case you 'lose' yours."

Perpetrator. I never thought I'd hear that word being used to describe *me*. Perpetrator of a poster, maybe. Not perpetrator of a crime.

I swear I feel like an ax murderer, even though I'm totally innocent. I would make the world's lousiest crook.

Which brings up the ultimate question: If I'm not doing it, who is?

I almost feel like I have to solve the mystery myself, just to get the sheriff off my back. The problem with mysteries is they're *mysterious*; if any bozo could figure them out, then they wouldn't be mysteries, would they?

So I think long and hard: Who's behind the swastikas? Who in this school could have a motive for doing something that's so upsetting to so many people?

It's such an awful thing to accuse a person of that I almost can't do it. As soon as I come up with a suspect, I think, no, not possible. I feel so bad that Sheriff Ocasek seems to think it's me that I hesitate to try to pin it on anybody else. Then I picture myself being blamed for something I absolutely didn't do, and I force myself to put together a list.

1. Christopher Solis is the first name that comes to my mind. He's just the worst kid in school, mean

to basically everybody. If in-school suspension gave frequent-flyer miles, he'd be in Bali by now, probably drawing swastikas on the beach. He picks on the art club, but I can't really take that personally, because he also picks on the science fair kids and the mathletes. He's an equal-opportunity moron with the disposition of a honey badger. Plus the whole town saw him whitewashing the curse words he painted on the parking lot of St. Basil's, so it's not like vandalism isn't already in his bag of tricks.

2. Clayton Pouncey. He's kind of an oddball. His dad is locally renowned as a jerk and a bigot, and there's a rumor that his grandfather was involved with the KKK and the Night of a Thousand Flames. A lot of people say that never happened. Pouncey isn't one of them, but he still has to be a prime suspect.

3. Jordie Duros. I've overheard him putting people down. It's usually not racist, but sometimes he gets pretty close to the line. I used to think he was just one of those popular kids who lets it go to his head. Then I heard that the swastika on the dumpster was painted in roofing tar. And everybody knows Jordie's family runs the only roofing business in town.

4. Caroline McNutt. This sounds crazy, and I'm probably wrong. Caroline doesn't have a racist bone in her body, and she's not a vandal, or any kind of evil person. But she's always talking about how brain-dead our school is, and how we have zero spirit and never

get involved the way other middle schools do. She practically lost her mind with happiness when the student council meeting got a decent turnout. Would she go so far as to paint swastikas just to rally the troops and get us all riled up to work on some project? Maybe not. But I can't rule it out.

5. The eighth graders. Well, not all of them, obviously. Still, whenever you hear grumbling about how tolerance education is worthless and what's so bad about a few swastikas, it almost always comes from them. True, eighth graders are pretty negative—I might be that way too next year. But Christopher Solis is an eighth grader. And Erick Federov, alpha jock, legend in his own mind. And Liza Guilfoyle, queen bee of the school. I'm just getting started here.

6. Mr. Kennedy. Who says Sheriff Ocasek is right that the "perp" has to be a kid? The custodian was in the building when the first swastika was painted. He could have done the deed and waited for someone to find it. And while I doubt Mr. Kennedy has a connection to the KKK or any hate groups, he is a pretty crabby guy. I almost don't blame him. Any time somebody barfs in the hall, or there's a food fight in the cafeteria, guess who has to clean it up. And let's face it, middle school students aren't the politest people on the planet. What if the swastikas have nothing to do with racism? What if they're Mr. Kennedy's way of getting even with us kids?

It's a lot of possibilities to juggle—especially for someone as busy as I am. Caroline appoints me official art director of the paper chain, which means I'm going to have to do most of it and supervise the rest. She makes herself project manager, positioning herself perfectly to boss people around, including me.

Mr. Brademas officially kicks off the paper chain on the morning announcements Thursday. By lunch, it's on everyone's lips. All anybody's talking about is how we're going to be up to our butts in paper links thanks to a kid named Link. That's what passes for comedy in this school. Caroline is complaining that the cool people get credit for everything around here. Like Link being popular has anything to do with what we're making our paper chain out of. Sometimes I worry about that girl.

If you're older than about six, you've probably made a paper chain or two in your life. It's not the hardest thing in the world to do. First, you take construction paper and cut it into strips about two inches wide and eight or nine inches long. You can do that with scissors, but it's a lot faster if you use those guillotine things schools have. Then you just glue the ends together so they form a loop. Presto, a link. You do the same thing with the next one, only this time you thread it through the first link. And so on until you hit six million, or until your fingers fall off.

We start after school. I'm impressed with the team that shows up—most of the art club, a lot of kids from the meeting, and about twenty sixth graders. You know how eighth graders are anti-everything? Well, sixth graders are the opposite of that. They're super gung ho, since being in middle school is still a big deal for them. Give them a year—they'll wise up.

I'm surprised to see Pouncey and Jordie among the crew, and I question whether I was wrong to put them on my suspect list. On the other hand, those two are tight with Link; where he goes, they usually follow. Besides, there's no law that says you can't paint swastikas and still be part of the group making a paper chain to fight against them. Actually, it could be the perfect plan to keep suspicion from falling on you.

Anyway, it's a good turnout. Almost too good, since we're bumping into each other in the art room. Even though we're making one giant paper chain, we've actually got about a dozen of them under construction. We'll hook everything into a single unit later on.

I'm expecting the usual art club squabbles—arguments over who's a cutter and who's a gluer, or whether it's too clashy to put orange next to red. This is different. Jordie refers to Pamela's designer yoga pants as leggings, and she storms out, ripping one of the chains under construction right down the middle. Pouncey refuses to work unless he's in charge of the guillotine, and he gets pretty obnoxious about it. Andrew slips in a puddle of spilled glue and knocks himself unconscious on the floor. By the time the nurse gets there to take him to the emergency room, his shirt is stuck to the tiles, and he has to be cut free with an X-Acto knife.

The sixth graders are determined to make more links than everybody else, so they skimp on the glue and their chain comes apart. One of them cries. Tabitha gets a paper cut and freaks out. Link gets on a Zoom bar mitzvah lesson, and we have to turn off the music so he can hear his rabbi. For the rest of the afternoon, we work to the tune of a Hebrew chant and Link struggling to repeat it.

Around five o'clock, kids start leaving to go home. Our production actually improves, since the art room isn't so crowded anymore and we're not getting in each other's way. Link's lesson ends, so we've got the music back on. It's even starting to be kind of fun when Pouncey comes running back from a bathroom break, his face grave.

"Guys—they found another swastika. It's burned into one of the lab tables in the science room. Mr. Kennedy says they used acid."

Caroline turns off the music, and we just stand there for a moment, looking at each other.

When I found that original swastika, I was terrified, almost like I believed it could peel itself off the wall and squeeze the life out of me like a boa constrictor. But, sad to say, we're used to them now. They make us feel helpless. Frustrated and angry. They create something in the pit of our stomachs that stirs up those emotions and more. And sure, fear is a part of it, but not the biggest part. Not anymore.

At first, I assume everyone is just going to leave. It's late, and the mood is definitely broken. But that's not what happens. Instead, we get back to work: silently, efficiently, and with purpose. The blade arm of Pouncey's guillotine moves like a piston. Dollops of glue land on colored paper, and fingers form loop after loop. Our chains grow faster and faster, until it seems as if we can churn out our six million in one day.

The swastika in the science room hasn't stopped us; it's

given us rocket fuel. The worst part of what's happening to us has always been that we have no way to fight back. Until now. *This* is how we fight back.

There's a cry of protest when Mr. Brademas comes to kick us out at six. He looks around the room, his eyes widening in surprise. "You've done all this? Amazing!"

It's almost like we're coming out of our trance and noticing it for the first time. Lengths of colorful paper chain hang from hooks all around the room. They pool onto the floor and stretch across tables.

"How many do you think we've got?" Link asks.

As art director, I've been keeping count in a notebook. I log in the last few links of production to make sure I'm up to date, and deliver the answer. "Nine hundred and seventy-three links."

It seems like an awful lot for just one day. But when six million is the number you're up against, it's pretty puny.

I do some quick calculating on my phone. "At this rate we'll reach six million in a little under seventeen years."

The sound of everybody's hopes deflating is almost a sucking inside the room.

"We'll never get there!" Jordie exclaims.

"I'll be, like, *thirty*!" Sophie muses mournfully.

"Remember what we talked about," Mr. Brademas puts in. "We're not going to get obsessed with the numbers. This is incredibly impressive, and it's only the first day. You should be proud of yourselves. *I'm* proud of you."

"Plus we're not the whole school," says Caroline, who always has something to add. "If we could get everybody working on this, who knows how high we could get?"

Everybody perks up.

"You all look exhausted," the principal informs us. "Go home, have a good dinner and a restful sleep. We'll get back to this tomorrow."

Out in the hall, I watch closely as Mr. Brademas locks the art room door. I know it's just a bunch of paper links, but for some reason, they feel really important.

CHAPTER THIRTEEN

DANA LEVINSON

One of the problems of living in Colorado is the time zone. When my friends in the east text me in the morning, my phone can start going off as early as five a.m. As scientists, Mom and Dad have a scientific solution: power down my phone at night.

Right. Like that's going to happen.

I'm fast asleep when the ping goes off. Delirious, I roll over and tap the screen. Yikes—5:53. I don't have to even open my eyes for two more hours. But they open on their own when I see that it's a text from my camp friend Angela in New York. We go to sleepaway together every summer.

> **CampAngie:** OMG! Just realized! I'm SO sorry!
> **DinoDana:** ????
> **CampAngie:** Chokecherry, Colorado! That's you, right?
> **DinoDana:** So?

In answer, she texts me a link. I click on it and it takes me to the YouTube channel of the vlogger ReelTok. His extreme close-up unibrow glares out at me, looking like it's been crammed into a too-small jam jar.

"Here's the latest from Chokecherry, swastika capital of Colorado. News flash: This idyllic American small town, where you can smell the apple pie cooling on the windowsill, used to be a hotbed for the KKK! We've been threatened with a lawsuit, TokNation, by the chamber of commerce of Chokecherry, Colorado. Why? For telling the truth! For daring to mention the Night of a Thousand Flames, when the entire town was encircled by burning crosses."

I click out of the video and stare at the conversation with Angela, suddenly aware that I'm breathing hard. Well, of course Angela thinks I'm trapped in a neo-Nazi horror town if ReelTok is her only source of information. But even in the middle of all this business with the swastikas, Chokecherry doesn't *feel* like a racist place. True, *somebody* must be racist—because the swastikas are obviously coming from somewhere. But most of the kids at school hate what's been happening. Every day, a larger number of volunteers show up to work on the paper chain. There are so many of us now that Caroline and Michael had to move production from the art room into the gym, and parts of the chain are draped over everything. You can barely see the climbing apparatus. We're already up over six thousand links.

But how can I explain all that to Angela? She's never lived in a place that didn't have a large Jewish community. So I text her back:

DinoDana: You can't believe everything you hear from Adam Tok.

CampAngie: But I'm worried about you! You're the only Jewish family in that town.

DinoDana: Not true. There's this one other kid

My finger freezes over the send button. Am I really saying what I think I'm saying?

DinoDana: He's studying for his bar mitzvah.

It's weird. Nothing is funny about Chokecherry. But for some reason, I'm laughing too hard to get back to sleep.

My father is still driving Ryan and me to school every morning. That's one ongoing effect of the swastikas no matter how many times I tell Angela everything's la-di-da.

"How's the paper chain coming along?" Dad asks after we drop Ryan at the elementary.

I'm surprised. "You know about that?"

"The school sent an email blast to all the families," he explains. "Interesting idea. As a parent, I'm behind it one hundred percent. As a scientist . . . well, the math doesn't exactly seem realistic."

"Yeah, Mr. Brademas reminds us of that about every eight seconds. It's supposed to be more about trying than succeeding."

"So long as you understand that," Dad confirms. "Because six million is an impossible task."

"The whole point," I tell him seriously, "is so we can see how big a number six million really is."

He goes kind of quiet digesting that. My dad's a smart guy, and it takes a lot to make him rethink something. This whole paper chain project is starting to get under my skin, in a good way.

There's a traffic jam at student drop-off. Caroline spread the word that the gym would be open early for paper-chaining, and I guess a lot of kids are taking her up on it. I strand Dad in the line of cars and run into the school.

The hall outside the gym is crowded with a mix of volunteers and spectators, and when I make it to the doors, I can see that the inside is a mob scene. It all revolves around Michael, who is standing at the center circle, clipboard in hand, shouting at Caroline.

"If the workers don't check in their output, then I can't count it! And if it doesn't get counted, how are we going to know how many we have?"

I can see what Michael's worried about. It's total chaos in the gym. There must be a hundred kids, probably more. Five of those guillotines—borrowed from the public library, the community college, plus our own elementary and high schools—slice construction paper with machine-like efficiency. No sooner have the strips been cut than fists fight over them. They're looped into shape and glued together, added to dozens of mini chains all around the room. Eventually, the mini chains are attached to bigger chains, as poor Michael scrambles around, desperately trying to keep up with the count.

I'm getting exhausted just watching it happen. It's impressive and a little bit scary at the same time. Spectators ring the gym, cheering on friends.

"Check out Sarah! Her hands are just a blur!"

"More glue! More glue!"

"Link and Jordie have the best crew! They're churning out chain twice as fast as anybody else!"

"Whoa—Oliver's bleeding all over the construction paper!"

"Too much glue!"

"What a waste of time! All this over a few swastikas!"

I feel like I'm on a leash, and somebody yanked it. Some tall eighth graders are standing behind me. I identify the speaker right away. This kid Erick Federov. He's supposedly the Link Rowley of the eighth grade, Mr. Popularity, basketball star.

I eavesdrop on their conversation. They're big complainers—"their" gym is being hogged by a bunch of do-gooders; where are they supposed to shoot around before school; sixth and seventh graders will volunteer for anything; blah, blah, blah. It's Erick who keeps bringing the topic back to two points: (1) the paper chain project is stupid, and (2) the swastikas are no big deal.

I must flinch, because they notice me.

"What's her problem?" I hear Erick whisper behind my back.

And one of his buddies supplies the answer. "That's Dana. You know, the Jewish girl."

Nothing's changed. I'm still watching the paper chain activity. But my neck is stiff, my jaw is clenched, and my good feeling about the project has turned to acid in my mouth. All I can think of is this is the town where the KKK found a home forty-plus years ago. This is the school someone is defacing with swastikas practically every day. For all I know, it's Erick himself, or one of his obnoxious friends.

The nine o'clock bell can't ring soon enough for me.

I sleepwalk through my morning classes. When I head for my locker to dump my books and get my lunch, Link is standing there waiting for me.

"Didn't see you in the gym this morning." He says it like it's an accusation.

"By the time I got there, you were all full up," I explain. "I figured I'd just get in the way."

That's when I notice that, in addition to his brown bag lunch, he's carrying a folder with Hebrew writing on it.

"So, I've started working on my bar mitzvah stuff," he tells me.

Well, *duh*—he spends every spare minute chanting away, trying to copy the prayers Rabbi Gold keeps sending him. He's at it in homeroom, the cafeteria, even while paper-chaining. The rabbi texts him audio clips, and Link follows along on papers with the Hebrew blessings spelled out phonetically. "And . . . ?" I prompt.

"It's harder than I thought. Because it's a whole other language and all that."

"Nobody's making you do it," I remind him.

He looks stubborn. "I'm making myself do it. It's important to me. And since you've already been mitzvahed—or whatever they call it—"

I fold my arms in front of me. "They call it *becoming a bat mitzvah*. It isn't something that happens to you, like getting struck by lightning."

"Anyway," he persists. "I figured you could help me out."

"A bar or bat mitzvah is the happiest day in a Jewish kid's life," I tell him. "You know why that is?"

"Well, it says on the internet that you get a lot of presents, but that doesn't really apply to me."

"It's not the presents. It's the fact that it's *over*. Done. And you don't have to do it ever again. So I can't help you, because the minute I finished my own, I deliberately erased every trace of it from my brain."

He doesn't smile. A Jewish kid would smile, but Link isn't your average Jewish kid.

"The problem is I've got no one else to ask," he says. "All my Jewish relatives—I mean, the ones I *would* have had—"

Never got a chance to be born, I finish in my head. The Holocaust took care of that. I feel lower than snail slime.

"I'm just kidding." I sigh. "I'll help you any way I can."

I wish the six hundred Link Rowley worshippers in this school could see their Big Man on Campus practically groveling with gratitude.

So I get my lunch and sit down at a secluded cafeteria table with the most popular boy in the seventh grade. For Hebrew lessons. Every girl in the big room stares in envy. If they only knew. Pamela and Sophie glare at me from their spot opposite Jordie and Pouncey, their eyes shooting sparks.

I wasn't lying about blocking my Hebrew education from memory, but it's amazing how fast it comes back. The prayers aren't quite songs, but there is kind of a chanting melody to them. I try to help Link with the tune, and he struggles to get the hang of it.

I have to say I'm a little bit impressed at how hard he's working. Part of me always believed that this whole bar mitzvah thing was kind of a goof for him. He has that reputation. The school halls echo with tales of his hilarious pranks, pulled off with the faithful Jordie and Pouncey at his side—the snowball-filled-with-peanut-butter caper; the salt-in-the-teachers'-room-coffee affair; the lard-in-the-parade-route incident. It's reached the level of legend around here. But Link seems to be 100 percent serious about learning his part for December 4. No matter how bad he does, he buries his face in his papers, cranks up Rabbi Gold on his phone, and gives it another try.

As we work, I notice that kids are getting up and rushing to the cafeteria windows. I peer outside, where a crowd is forming on the front walk. My heart sinks. Another swastika. It was only a matter of time before somebody stuck one right on the front of the school, where it's impossible to hide it.

I look again. The spectators are gathered around a short, youngish man who is walking from his car, which is parked in the no parking zone where the buses pick up and drop off. He looks kind of familiar, but I can't quite place him. Whoever he is, he seems to be a big draw. Kids are swarming all around him, coming from every door in the school. There are even a few teachers out there, trying—unsuccessfully—to herd their students back inside.

Link is oblivious to this, still buried in his bar mitzvah.

I tap him on the shoulder. "Do you recognize that guy out front? The one pulling the tripod out of his car?"

His brow furrows for a moment, then his eyes widen. "Is that ReelTok?"

"No way!" But it occurs to me that I've never seen the real Adam Tok—just the letterbox view from the top of the eyebrows to the bottom of the lower lip. I squint to squeeze his face into the tiny frame I'm used to on YouTube. The unibrow seals the deal. "You're right!"

"But what's ReelTok doing here?" Link asks in amazement.

I know the answer to that. "He's here for our swastikas! He's been making a big deal out of it for a couple of weeks now. I'll bet he came to get a story for his YouTube channel. Look—he's setting up a camera!"

"It's my fault," Link admits. "I showed my dad ReelTok screaming about Chokecherry, and now the chamber of commerce is threatening to sue him. Let's get out there."

We run through the cafeteria doors and join the throng around the famous vlogger. Besides the claustrophobic rectangle of face he shows the online world, Adam Tok is compact and squat, with curly black hair and stick-out ears. He's casually dressed in jeans and a sweatshirt and, for some reason, authentic leather cowboy boots with gigantic heels that boost him up to merely short.

He's speaking into his camera when we get there. "It took

a four-hour plane ride and three hours of driving on mountain roads, but here I am in God's country, Anytown, USA. I haven't seen any swastikas yet, but have faith, TokNation. Chokecherry won't let us down." He pauses the recording and surveys the crowd. "Is there a Caroline McNutt here?"

"That's me!" Caroline pushes her way to the front. "Mr. Tok, on behalf of the student council—"

He cuts her off. "Show me this paper chain you've been posting on Instagram."

"Oh, sure," Caroline enthuses. "We're working on it in the gym—"

Mr. Brademas storms across the lawn and confronts the vlogger. "You have no right to photograph my students. You can't use those pictures without permission, and believe me, you won't get it."

ReelTok holds out his hand. "I'm Adam Tok—"

The principal's face flames red. "I know exactly who you are, Mr. Tok, and you're not welcome to come here and exploit our problems. This is the real world, not YouTube. You need a permit to film on school property. And if that's your vehicle, I regret to inform you it's illegally parked."

Halfway through this speech, the blogger turns on his camera and swivels it toward Mr. Brademas. "Here's Nicholas Brademas, principal of Swastika Middle School, trespassing on freedom of the press," he narrates.

"Students," Mr. Brademas addresses us. "Get inside the school. Immediately."

A few kids start to straggle back to the building, but most

of us just stand there, fascinated. The principal may be in charge, but ReelTok is a *celebrity*.

A police car is coming up the street followed by a tow truck marked CHOKECHERRY DEPARTMENT OF PUBLIC WORKS. Mr. Brademas hurries to the curb to confer with the officer.

The blogger is about to get his car towed, and maybe even be arrested, but it doesn't seem to bother him much. I guess when your job is to get attention on the internet, all publicity is good publicity.

"Come on," Link tells me. "Let's go do some more work on my bar mitzvah."

"Bar mitzvah?" ReelTok pulls a notebook from his pocket. "My research shows only one Jewish student at this school, and it's a girl."

"It's kind of a long story," Link explains.

The blogger beams at him. "I like long stories."

There's a loud clunk as the tow truck operator hooks a chain to ReelTok's rental car.

The blogger pulls his camera off the tripod and makes sure to get the whole thing on video.

"That's what I love about small towns," he narrates. "Everyone's so friendly."

CHAPTER FOURTEEN

REELTOK

From the YouTube channel of Adam Tok

Interview with Lincoln Rowley

REELTOK: Rowley . . . Rowley. Any relation to George Rowley from the Chokecherry Chamber of Commerce? He's planning to sue me, you know.

LINK: Yeah, sorry about that. He's my dad.

REELTOK: Don't apologize. I love being sued. It gets me headlines. I love headlines. Headlines mean followers, and followers mean ka-ching, ka-ching

LINK: He gets really touchy about anything that makes the town look bad.

REELTOK: Like an army of screwballs in sheets burning crosses.

LINK: That was a long time ago. Some people say it never happened.

REELTOK: I'd think you'd have a stronger opinion on that, considering you're Chokecherry's newest Jewish citizen.

LINK: Yeah, should I tell the audience about my grandmother and the Holocaust?

REELTOK: TokNation is more than just an audience. They're TokNation because they see through the idiotic phony blabbery of a world that's ninety-eight percent baloney. I already told your grandmother's story in my last video. So, Lincoln—

LINK: People call me Link.

REELTOK: Like the links in your famous paper chain! Not for nothing, but my video about the paper chain got quite a response from TokNation. But why don't you tell us a little about this pretend bar mitzvah you've been planning?

LINK: It's not pretend. It's with a real rabbi in a real temple in Shadbush Crossing. My friend Dana has been helping me learn my part. She's Jewish too.

REELTOK: I've got big news, Link. I've already talked to Rabbi Gold, and ReelTok will be live-streaming your bar mitzvah to TokNation and the entire world on December fourth! What do you have to say to that?

LINK: Wow, awesome. Kind of scary, though. If I mess up, millions of people are going to know.

REELTOK: Only the ones who speak Hebrew.

LINK: I guess. Still, I was nervous already. But this will be like being on TV.

REELTOK: Piece of cake for a kid with guts like yours. After all, you picked a pretty scary time to be Jewish in Chokecherry, Colorado, with so many swastikas popping up at your school. And even after all these weeks, nobody knows who's doing it. Does that make you want to reconsider your decision?

LINK: Not really. You don't pick who you are. You just *are*.

CHAPTER FIFTEEN

CAROLINE MCNUTT

I deserve this.

Ever since I was four, when I tried to organize my fellow preschoolers into going on strike for better cookies at snack time, I've had the same problem. Apathy. Nobody cares. Sure, they'll go to a dance or a party. But they won't lift a finger to organize one. And if that means it never happens, that's just fine with them too.

I've been in student government since the first grade. Getting anybody to join a club, or volunteer for a committee, or do anything at all is like having your teeth pulled out one at a time by needle-nose pliers.

Until now.

The paper chain project is a student government dream come true. Picture all the student participation I haven't been able to drum up over the years cashing in at the same time— with interest.

You should see the gym. No, scratch that. You *can't* see the gym—not much of it anyway. It's a paper chain jungle. Michael says we're up over sixty thousand links, and lengths of chain hang everywhere, doubled, tripled, and quadrupled up. When the volunteers come, it's wall-to-wall people.

I watch the whole thing in motion—everybody busy; hundreds of kids banding together, working side by side to accomplish a single, worthwhile goal. Sometimes I'm so overcome with gratitude that I have to remind myself: This is my reward for all those years of begging and pleading, trying to whip up enthusiasm and getting nowhere.

I guess it's a shame that it took swastikas to inspire the kids of Chokecherry to get up off their butts. But the end result is more than worth it. For the first time in my life, I'm proud of my school. A bad thing happened to us—is *still* happening to us. And we turned it into the ultimate good thing, times a million.

Not only that, but we're getting kind of famous. Now that he's here in town, ReelTok is vlogging about our school full-time. A lot of the local big shots—like Mr. Brademas, Mayor Radisson, and Mr. Rowley—aren't too thrilled about it. It doesn't reflect well on Chokecherry that somebody has been putting swastikas all over the school and we can't catch who's doing it.

The adults hate ReelTok so much that they won't even let him onto school grounds. But Mr. Tok is pretty sharp. On his show yesterday, he said, "I've been thrown out of the White House by the Secret Service. I've been banned from Buckingham Palace by the beefeaters. Taylor Swift sicced her dog on me. The commander at West Point threatened me with a flamethrower. What do I care that some small-town principal doesn't want me in his school? LOL."

So he sets himself up in the little park across the street. He knows exactly how close to the campus he's legally allowed to be, and he's three inches past that, so the police can't touch him. He's got a giant beach umbrella and a folding chair with a cup holder that always has a Big Gulp from 7-Eleven, who lets him use their bathroom. And there's usually a lineup of kids who can't wait to be interviewed.

"Students," Mr. Brademas tells us on the morning announcements, "I urge you all to stay away from the individual known as ReelTok. He's only interested in sensationalizing the problems we've been having in order to attract viewers to his vlog. He's presenting our school and our town in the worst possible light. The last thing any of us should be doing is helping him accomplish that."

That day, the lineup in front of ReelTok's tripod is twice as long. Who can resist the chance to be on one of the most popular channels on YouTube?

The principal's right that ReelTok is pretty harsh in his videos about the swastikas. In his opinion, we're either racist or stupid—stupid because our police can't find one lousy kid, racist because maybe they're not really looking. And the blogger never misses a chance to remind everybody that Chokecherry was once a hotbed of KKK activity. He mentions the Night of a Thousand Flames in every posting.

My mother thinks the problem with ReelTok is he's too negative. "If he's so interested in our town, he should be telling the world about the good things that are going on here. Like our annual mac-and-cheese-eating contest. That raised a lot of money for charity. Or the dinosaur dig in the mountains.

The university says it might turn out to be one of the biggest finds in history. Why does everything have to be about swastikas?"

I don't even try to explain it to Mom. Swastikas are *news*. And swastika news means paper chain news. Mr. Tok hasn't actually seen the paper chain, since he's banned from school property. But I texted him some pictures, and I'm glad I did. He used them in a few videos, and you wouldn't believe the response. On ReelTok's website, there are already more comments about our paper chain than any other topic. People *love* it. Sure, there are a few cranks who think the idea is stupid, or that we ripped it off from the paper clip school in Tennessee. Some say the whole thing is a waste of time, because we'll never reach six million. But the vast majority are pro–paper chain. They say it's the perfect response to the swastikas in our school. A lot of the messages come from middle school kids all over the country, encouraging us to keep working and never give up. Which is what we're going to do. This is the kind of activity student government was born to do.

So when I hear my name on the PA system being called to the principal's office, I'm psyched. It's been nothing but good news ever since this project started. I know for a fact that Chokecherry Middle School has never seen this level of participation for an extracurricular activity. Even Mr. Brademas has to admit that the negative of the swastikas has been turned around by the positive of the paper chain. I figure at minimum I'm about to get a pat on the back. Who knows, for an achievement like this, I might even be elevated from seventh-grade president to president of everybody. I can't help grinning at the thought of Daniel Faraz's face when he gets *that* news.

So I'm a little confused by the look of sympathy on the secretary's face when she shows me into Mr. Brademas's office. Michael is already there, sitting very small in a chair, looking devastated. The principal is gray-faced and grim. What's going on? We've got the hottest middle school activity in the country right now, and everybody's acting like this is a funeral!

I perch at the end of the empty chair, and Mr. Brademas gets right to the point. "I can't commend you enough for what you've accomplished with the paper chain project. To reach sixty thousand links is impressive enough. To manage it so quickly is astounding. It makes it all the more difficult to have to bring it to a close."

"A *close*?" My heart practically busts through my rib cage. "You mean stop? Why? We're kicking *butt*—I mean, it's going so well—"

"Too well," the principal says. "In fact, we've run out of construction paper."

"Can't we borrow some from the other schools?" Even as I'm asking the question, I see Michael shaking his head sadly.

"We already have," the principal informs me. "We've used every scrap of construction paper in the whole district. And there's no money in the budget to purchase more."

"We can fundraise!" I squeak. "We'll sell raffle tickets! And scented candles! And chocolate bars! I'll sell my bike! I'll do anything! Please don't cancel the paper chain!"

"Sorry, Caroline. It's already done."

And just like that, it's over—the greatest student government project in the history of school. Believe me, I don't let it go that easily. I offer to go door-to-door for donations and pass the hat around the cafeteria. I beg and whine and even cry a little. What's so hard about raising money? The principal's gold cuff links alone would bring in hundreds! But he's a mule, and eventually, I'm so upset that I don't know what I'm saying anyway.

Out in the hall, Michael tries to cheer me up. "It was pretty cool while it lasted. We've got a lot to be proud of."

"Don't you dare make me feel better!" I snap. "What kind of message are we sending? Swastikas are bad—but only till you run out of paper to fight against them? And now that we're broke, they're okay? How's that something to be proud of?"

"Well, I don't think Mr. Brademas meant it that way—" he offers.

I stomp away from him. I refuse to spend my time with anybody who doesn't think this is the end of the world. If I have to listen to a guy putting a positive spin on this, my head is probably going to explode. At this moment, I want nothing but gloom, despair, negativity, and complaining.

But where am I going to find that?

CHAPTER SIXTEEN

REELTOK

From the YouTube channel of Adam Tok

Interview with Caroline McNutt

REELTOK: A special treat, TokNation—we welcome Caroline McNutt to the little slice of Chokecherry I haven't been kicked out of yet. It was Caroline's Instagram that first introduced me to the paper chain.

CAROLINE: I can't talk to you. Mr. Brademas told us all to stay away from ReelTok.

REELTOK: So why are you here?

CAROLINE: Because Mr. Brademas is a—sorry. I'm seventh-grade president. I should set an example.

REELTOK: I think you have something to say.

CAROLINE: No. Yes. The paper chain . . . it's canceled.

REELTOK: Interesting. So somebody in that school doesn't think that standing up to racism and anti-Semitism is a good idea.

CAROLINE: That's not the reason. We just ran out of paper. And the principal says there's no money in the budget to buy more. I always knew it would be hard to get to six million links, but I never thought the reason would be the school board going cheapo on us!

REELTOK: It's all about priorities. People call New York a cesspool, but New Yorkers would never knuckle under to intolerance and let some lowlife get away with drawing swastikas.

CAROLINE: Nobody's letting anybody get away with anything. We just can't find out who it is.

REELTOK: Who do you think is doing it?

CAROLINE: How should I know? I'm just a kid.

REELTOK: You're the seventh-grade president. Don't you know your own school?

CAROLINE: I know the kids in my school never got involved in anything until the paper chain came along. It seems to me that if schools spend money on field trips and football equipment, they should spend just as much on something that's a million times more important.

REELTOK: You go, girl! Don't hold back! TokNation wants to hear it!

CAROLINE: Seriously! You see all these TV shows about kids being at their worst. Well, here's an example of kids at their best. And what do the adults do? They shut us down! It's so unfair!

REELTOK: Yeah! Especially when you consider the adults we're talking about.

CAROLINE: Wait—what?

REELTOK: The mayor and his police force, who should be finding whoever's behind the swastikas instead of hassling an innocent blogger. This guy Rowley from the chamber of commerce, who wants to sue me. Your own principal, who's shutting down the paper chain—and that's after doing everything in his power to keep me from telling your story to TokNation and the world. There's nothing wrong with you, Caroline. You have every right to be ticked off at the adults of Chokecherry. Just like they moved heaven and Earth to keep a lid on the Night of a Thousand Flames, they're silencing you.

CAROLINE: You came here all the way from New York. Do you even like our town?

CHAPTER SEVENTEEN

CLAYTON POUNCEY

I think Link Rowley having a bar mitzvah is the stupidest thing I've ever heard in my life.

Then again, I think most things are stupid, so you probably shouldn't go by me.

The guy's about as Jewish as I am. Not that I'm a big expert. I don't know anybody Jewish except Dana Levinson, and she's annoying. That has nothing to do with her being Jewish. All the egglets are annoying. They show up here in their electric cars with their kale salad and complain about how our town is too backward to ban plastic bags. If their folks are such geniuses, how come they spend their days rooting around in the mud? I did that when I was three. Mud is mud, regardless of whether there are dinosaur bones underneath it.

That's kind of the rule with me. *Things* are stupid. *People* are annoying.

Anyway, I get the whole sob story with Link's grandmother. I've met her a bunch of times. She's nice. Once, when we were little, she took Link, Jordie, and me to meet Santa at the Shadbush County Mall. If Link is doing this to please her, then he's barking up the wrong tree.

Come to think of it, what tree *is* he barking up? Why's he

doing this? Because of the swastikas? Everybody has to look at those, and no one else decided to have a bar mitzvah. Because he suddenly got religion? He's not the type. He's a goofball, like Jordie and me. A troublemaker and proud of it. And even if he did see the light—or whatever you call it—why not stick with the religion he already has?

This is what happens when you let yourself get too mixed up with family. Link hears one sad story about a grandparent, and he's lost his mind. We Pounceys have grandparent stories too. I don't remember much about Grandpa, but the word is he wore a white sheet with a hood—and supposedly that wasn't even the nastiest thing about him. When I find myself focusing on him, I change my focus to something else ASAP. Sunflower seeds, usually, because I love sunflower seeds. But anything works—video games, my locker combination, bait. Anything but the fact that one of my best friends has developed a whole new life without me.

I barely recognize the kid anymore. Used to be that Link, Jordie, and I could kill a whole afternoon lying around, planning our next big gag. The details we'd go into—you'd think we were planning to take over the White House and kick out the president. That doesn't happen anymore. Every spare minute is filled with bar mitzvah stuff. We go to Dairy Queen, and while they're making our cones, Link pulls out his phone for a few extra minutes of Rabbi Gold chanting in Hebrew. You know how in languages like Spanish and French, you can pick out a word here or there because it sounds kind of like English?

Not Hebrew. Everybody looks at us like we're nuts. *We're* not. It's just Link.

"What does all that mean?" I ask him.

"It's the blessing over a goblet of wine," Link tells us.

"Really?" Jordie's amazed. "What's the drinking age for Jewish?"

"You don't actually get any," Link informs him with a grin. "It's just part of the ceremony."

"And afterward you get to stomp on the glass," Jordie adds. "I saw that in movie once."

"That's for weddings, not bar mitzvahs," Link explains.

I googled *bar mitzvah* back when I first found out Link was having one. There was a lot of stuff about becoming a man. I don't see how putting on a suit and singing in a foreign language makes you that, but whatever. In the Pouncey family, becoming a man usually involves shooting something. For all I know, in Grandpa's time, it might even have meant shooting some*one*. You never knew with Grandpa.

Sunflower seeds . . . love those sunflower seeds . . .

"When you do the thing—you know, the mitzvah," I ask, "are they going to make you wear that little beanie hat?"

"It's called a kippah. Rabbi Gold says it's optional at Temple Judea," Link replies, "but I think I might wear it."

Jordie nods. "Go big or go home."

The lady hands us our cones, and we sit at a table.

"To be honest, guys," Link says between slurps, "if you ask me why I'm doing this, I don't know if I can explain it, even to myself. My mom's weird about it. My dad's rolling with it, but I'm pretty sure he'd throw me a parade if I'd give it up."

I'm no one to talk, but Link's old man is kind of a piece of work. If the point of all this is to get Mr. Rowley to loosen the reins, maybe it isn't as stupid as I thought.

"Wouldn't you know it?" I complain. "They put all the sprinkles on one side of my cone. But I can't go up and demand more because they'll say I already licked it."

"You already did," Jordie reminds me.

"You know what?" Link puts in. "*This* is why I'm having a bar mitzvah."

Jordie frowns. "Because Pouncey got ripped off on sprinkles?"

"Because our whole lives are based on dumb stuff," Link insists. "Like who didn't get enough sprinkles, or what girl just checked us out."

"Checked *you* out," I grumble.

"Seriously—those things are fine, but they're not, you know, important. So when I found out that stuff about my grandmother, I wasn't sure what to do. But I couldn't just do nothing."

"If sprinkles aren't important," I tell him, "how about we swap cones?"

"No way! You already licked yours," Link snaps. Then he grabs his phone and turns on Rabbi Gold again.

It's enough to turn the ice cream to poison in my stomach.

School's messed up too. Part of that's the swastikas, obviously. But most of the fuss is about the paper chain project, which is off because we ran out of paper. Everybody's going ape because who could have predicted that you need paper to make a paper chain?

I personally think the paper chain is stupid and most of the people who are losing their minds over it are annoying. But it was something to do—and it was kind of cool at the end of the day when Michael announced how many links we were up to. That's assuming he did a real count, instead of just saying any old number. That kid's even more annoying than the rest of them.

The only part I'm going to miss is my guillotine. I freaked when I found out that it's called that. I always wanted my own guillotine. I was an executioner . . . of paper anyway. But as I mentioned, that's all in the past.

The project may be in the past, but the chain itself is very much in the present, all 61,472 links of it. It's draped over everything in the gym, even spiraling up and down the climbing ropes. PE classes have to be held outside, rain or shine. At some point, the school is going to have to throw it out, or recycle it, or something that makes it go away. But if Brademas and the teachers are planning to do that, they haven't mentioned it to us kids yet. I think they're afraid that if they try it, the cry of outrage is going to echo off the mountains. Caroline is passing around a petition to protect the links we've already got. I signed. Why not?

Even if you're not near the gym, where you can see the

miles of paper links, your phone is always blowing up with notifications that ReelTok has posted another video about it. I can't believe I used to be a fan of that guy. He's always funny and cool when you watch him on YouTube. But when he's on a folding chair across from your school, sucking on a Slurpee and talking to himself, he's kind of annoying.

Then comes the day that Mr. Brademas gets the idea that the paper chain isn't such a big deal anymore, and he can finally get it out of his school.

The first I hear of it, I'm heading for my locker at lunch when a half-crazed female voice shrieks, *What are you doing?*

I peer in the gym door in time to see Caroline grabbing a scissors away from Mr. Kennedy's reach a split second before he was about to cut a length of paper chain off the climbing apparatus. Mr. Kennedy is too shocked to react, but there are a couple of other custodians with him, also with scissors. A strand of links is already lying on the floor.

"No-o-o-o-o-o!!!"

I have to flatten myself to my locker to avoid being trampled. Kids are coming from all directions, stampeding through the hall, to investigate the source of the disturbance. Seeing the paper chain in danger galvanizes them into action.

Nobody actually pushes the custodians out of the gym. But so many people rush to protect the paper chain at the same time that the mass of kids bubbles through the door, carrying the three men with it. Mr. Kennedy is already shouting into his walkie-talkie as the wave carries him by me.

"We've got a situation here—"

By the time the first few teachers make it onto the scene, they find total chaos. The hallway is packed with kids, all frantic, all babbling at the same time. A wall of bodies blocks both gym entrances.

Mr. Slobodkin is outraged. "You have classes to go to!"

Nobody moves because nobody hears him. Or if they do, they don't care. It's nothing new for me; I never care what teachers say. But for everyone else it's pretty different. This is turning into an interesting day.

Mrs. Babbitt claps her hands. "Let's move, people!"

No response. Arms are folded over chests. The message is clear. It's like they say on *Monty Python*: None shall pass.

Hustling through the throng comes the big enchilada himself: Brademas. On the ticked-off scale from one to ten, he's at least an eleven.

"Break it up!" he bellows.

I'm not a Caroline fan, but give her props. She doesn't back down a millimeter. "First you have to promise not to throw away the paper chain!"

The principal is so shocked at being challenged by his own seventh-grade president that he backs away from her, stepping on my foot. Spying me, he seems amazed that disobedience is happening and I'm not a part of it. "Good for you, Clayton," he tells me. "I'm happy to see that you have the sense to stay out of this."

It's the wrong thing to say to a guy like me. No one accuses a Pouncey of staying out of trouble. So I step forward and join Caroline at the human wall.

Now Brademas is bright red. "The paper chain project is

over. This is a school. We can't sacrifice our gym indefinitely because a few people are disappointed."

In my defense, I only say the thing I say next to stick it to Brademas. But the instant it's out of my mouth, I'm blown away that it came from me. "Those aren't just loops of paper in there! Those links represent people who died in the Holocaust. You can't just chuck that like it's nothing!"

"Yeah!" Caroline exclaims. It's the first time she's ever agreed with me. I must be doing something wrong.

Still, I can feel the wall of kids stiffening around me. There's even a smattering of applause.

"That's ridiculous!" The principal is getting louder. "We all knew there was no chance of reaching six million links. And even if we could, the school district would never approve that much money just for paper!"

At that moment, Link and Jordie come sprinting in from outside. They're a little confused by the mob scene at the gym entrance. But when they spy the principal, the news pours out of them.

"Mr. Brademas, come quick!" Link exclaims. "The guy needs you to sign!"

The principal frowns. "Sign what?"

"There's a truck outside," Jordie pants. "And it's full of construction paper!"

"I didn't order any construction paper!" Brademas snaps.

"It's not an order," Link explains breathlessly. "It's a donation! This art supply company—they heard about our paper chain on ReelTok! They want to help us finish it!"

The principal makes some comment, but the cheer that goes up in the hallway drowns out everything. If a giant meteor had hit the football field, we wouldn't have heard that either. Kids are jumping up and down and cheering. Caroline throws her arms around Brademas and hugs him—like she wasn't just yelling at the guy two seconds ago. I award the principal a booming slap on the back—because, hey, when am I ever going to get another chance to do that?

The best part is that Brademas obviously wants the whole paper chain thing to be over, and now he's lost his only excuse for killing it. He looks like a guy who took a big bite of something really gross and missed his chance to spit it out. Now everybody's looking at him, and he has no choice but to swallow it.

Did I say the paper chain is stupid?

Scratch that. It's starting to grow on me.

CHAPTER EIGHTEEN

LINCOLN ROWLEY

The first TV crew comes to Chokecherry on the Saturday my father takes me suit shopping for my bar mitzvah.

We go to Jerome's on Main Street—as head of the chamber of commerce, Dad never lets us buy anything at the Shadbush County Mall, which is outside the town limits. I try on a plain navy blue suit. It isn't as cool as the shiny black one I first picked out, but as my father puts it, "This is a bar mitzvah, not a funeral."

Every time Dad says *bar mitzvah*, he looks like he's just taken a swig of vinegar. But I give him full credit. For the first time ever, he's going through with something for my sake . . . or maybe because Mom told him he has to. He's bringing in floral arrangements to decorate the synagogue on the big day, and he's paying for the congregational Kiddush, which is like a mini lunch after the service is over. He's even warming up to Rabbi Gold, now that he's found out, through our Zoom calls, that the rabbi is a fellow Denver Broncos fan.

Speaking of the Zooms, Rabbi Gold has explained all the parts of the service to me so I'll know what to expect on December 4. We've also spent a lot of time discussing what being Jewish means to him—not just the religion part, but the fight for social justice. Jewish people have been the underdogs so often that they understand what it's like to be an underdog. I can't help thinking of the sports connection—like when a team nobody takes seriously comes together for a playoff push. But so many times in Jewish history, what was at stake was a lot more than a trophy or a championship. It was survival.

We've talked a lot about what my grandmother's family must have gone through. Yeah, I learned about the Holocaust in school—both in fifth grade and in tolerance education. But it's way more real to me now that I have this direct relation. Rabbi Gold says becoming a bar mitzvah is taking some of that history on my shoulders. That scares me a little, because I'm not sure I deserve to be trusted with something so heavy. But the rabbi says I'm practicing ten times as hard as most of his other bar mitzvah students, and that I'm asking ten times as many questions. That has to count for something.

Putting on a suit makes me feel even more out of my element, like I've left the world of greasing the parade route and shoving fertilizer through a mail slot and moved on to a place where everything is more serious. I don't know how I feel about it.

Dad's eyes widen a little when I come out of the changing room. "Wow, kid. When did you grow shoulders?" He steps forward and adjusts my lapels.

"It feels like I'm wearing broken glass," I tell him honestly. "And the shirt collar is strangling me."

"You kids today—anything more fitted than pajamas is formalwear. My mom used to put me in a jacket and tie every Sunday for church."

The word hangs in the air between us—*church* as opposed to the synagogue we're buying this suit for.

"Thanks, Dad," I say finally. "I know this is something you never thought you'd be doing."

"You got that right. But hey, I hear the Levinson girl says you're pretty good."

I shrug out of the jacket and put it back on the hanger. "I don't know about 'good.' I'm trying."

"You'll get there. Any son of mine having a bar mitzvah is going to nail it. Giving a hundred and ten percent, no matter *what* you're doing—that's a good sign for your future. But if you change your mind, you don't have to go through with this."

I regard him sharply. "Why would I change my mind?"

He shrugs. "You're young. Kids your age do things on impulse all the time. For all I know, you've had second thoughts, but you're too embarrassed to admit it. I get that it'll be a little awkward to tell your friends the bar mitzvah's off—"

"But it's *not* off," I interrupt. "This isn't about getting attention or making a point. I *need* to do this!"

Dad turns to the tailor. "I guess we'll take the suit."

The tailor makes a few more measurements and gives me a lecture about not having a growth spurt. I promise to do my best, and we get out of there with a ticket to pick up the suit next week.

"Should we grab lunch while we're in town?" Dad asks as we leave the store.

"Can't," I reply. "I promised Jordie I'd go over and cheer him up. Pamela broke up with him, so he's kind of bumming."

"I had no idea seventh graders have anything to break up from," Dad puts in, surprised.

"Get a clue, Dad." He has to be the only person in town who doesn't know Jordie and Pamela have been on-again, off-again since second grade.

That's when I spot the TV crew. Their van is hard to miss, with the satellite dish on the roof and the splashy logo of one of the Denver stations painted on the side. They've got a reporter on the street interviewing people.

I can almost feel Dad's spine stiffening. On the one hand, there's nothing he loves more than getting publicity for our town. But it has to be positive publicity, and these days, Chokecherry's claim to fame is the paper chain. In my father's mind, that's not good. Follow the paper chain and it will take you to the swastikas. Follow the swastikas and you'll eventually arrive back in the seventies with the KKK. And that's a huge stain for the whole area.

A lot has happened with the paper chain since that truck-load of construction paper arrived at school. It turns out that canceling the project was the best thing that ever could have happened to it. When you take something away, that's all anybody ever wants—especially with ReelTok posting video after video accusing Chokecherry of silencing its kids because the town doesn't have the guts to face up to its racist history. So when Mr. Brademas gave us the okay to start paper-chaining again, we took off like a rocket.

It's not just the volunteers anymore. Practically the whole school is in on it now. The art teachers signed on first, followed by the social studies teachers, so now paper links are under construction all day, not just before and after school and at lunch. We never knew the elementary school was helping us until their custodian drove up to the loading bay with the payload of his truck overflowing with chain. The high school signed on next—anything the little kids could do, they could do better. Families are paper-chaining at home. So are the residents of Mountain View Retirement Village. Caroline got her parents to take some of our paper to the community room at the YMCA, so production from there comes over every evening when they close.

By the end of the first week, our gym was so jam-packed that the next link anybody tried to cram in there would have blown the roof off. So the owner of Shadbush County Farm Equipment lets us use his empty warehouse for paper chain storage. Kostakis Brothers Trucking sent three giant dump trucks to move everything from gym to warehouse free of charge. It's not just our school anymore. It's not even just kids. It's like the whole town has bought into our project, and if you're not cutting and gluing, you're finding other ways to help. Even the local restaurants are sending over snacks and drinks.

"Yeah, that's him! That's the bar mitzvah kid over there!"

Suddenly, fingers are pointing in my direction, and the reporter and her crew are heading our way. Beside me, Dad groans.

Ever since I did that interview with ReelTok, everybody knows about my bar mitzvah. And even though it really has nothing to do with the paper chain, people seem to put the two together. I can sort of understand it. The paper chain is about the Holocaust, so there's a Jewish connection. And a bar mitzvah is totally Jewish, even when it's a guy like me who's having one.

The microphone is shoved in my face. "Lincoln Rowley— will you answer a few questions for *Denver Action News*?"

I catch a pleading look from Dad, who's dying for me to say no. But he doesn't interfere when I agree.

"Talk about how the paper chain project inspired you to explore your Jewish heritage."

I try to explain that I found out about Mom's family first and the paper chain came later, but they don't really want to hear that. It's the same thing when you're dealing with Adam Tok. Reporters have a way of turning your story into what they want it to be. For ReelTok, the theme is: Kids force their town to confront its racist past. For Denver TV, the message seems to be: Paper chain good. Therefore all good things must come from paper chain. When the sun rises tomorrow, it'll be thanks to the paper chain.

Eventually, Dad interjects gently, "I think that's enough bar mitzvah talk for now. Link doesn't want to hog the spotlight away from the paper chain or our world-famous dinosaur dig. Did you know there's a major fossil discovery right outside Chokecherry?"

The reporter doesn't take the bait. "All right. I think we have enough footage. How about you direct us to the school so we can get some shots of the chain itself?"

"The paper chain isn't at the school," I tell them. "It got

too big. We had to move it over to Shadbush County Farm Equipment."

Poor Dad. Not only does *Denver Action News* ignore his dinosaur dig, but the next thing he knows, he's driving across town, leading their mobile unit to the paper chain he never wanted them to focus on in the first place.

The sliding doors of the warehouse are wide open, and I catch a glimpse of the kaleidoscope of color inside. There are plenty of kids around, pushing shopping carts and wheelbarrows, and pulling wagons piled high with chain. As we park, a sixth grader wheels by on a bicycle, a clear plastic trash bag of links over his shoulder. Michael stands at the door like a sentry, clipboard in hand, checking in all the new arrivals, faithfully keeping the count. Yesterday we passed four hundred thousand, but the number has to be even higher than that now.

The mobile unit pulls up beside us, and the crew scrambles for cameras and equipment to capture this beehive of activity.

Dad slumps in the driver's seat. "Greatest dinosaur find in fifty years and I can't get anybody to pay attention. But a warehouse full of scrap paper is front-page news."

Among the comings and goings, I spy Pamela and Pouncey leaving the building. If she's trying to make Jordie jealous, she's picked the wrong guy. Pouncey is about as romantic as an orange traffic cone. I also happen to know that he finds her annoying.

Dad and I follow the camera crew into the warehouse . . . and it's almost as if we've crashed into an invisible barrier.

My father's hand squeezes my shoulder. I feel my jaw drop halfway to the floor.

Yeah, okay, it packed the school gym pretty much full. But this is an astounding sight. The cavernous storage space is already half full with mounds of paper links. The expanse of bright colors is so gigantic that my eyes almost can't process it in one sweep. Every time I think I've seen it all, I turn in a new direction, and there's another huge mountain. I stand at the entrance to the building, blinking, struggling to take it in. It's hard to imagine that this landscape of loops was made one link at a time, starting that afternoon in the art room.

The camera guy almost loses his balance trying to pan the vastness of it.

Even Dad is impressed. "Incredible! There must be miles of it!"

Michael supplies the answer. "Twenty-eight miles," he says. "You know, estimating about four inches per link."

The TV crew makes him say it again on camera.

Twenty-eight miles. And this is barely a fraction of the six million we're shooting for. I feel a surge of pride—until I remember what the number six million really represents. I go cold all over, thinking of Grandma's family. *My* family.

The reporter points to a catwalk just under the high ceiling. "Go up there and get a panoramic view," she tells her cameraman. "We have to see just how huge all this is."

So up he goes to the wrought-iron perch and begins a slow pan across the sea of multicolored chain. Everyone follows the camera lens as it moves across the warehouse floor and comes to a sudden stop.

"What's the problem?" she calls.

The man's voice is reedy. "You're going to want to take a look at this."

We head up the metal staircase—the reporter, Michael, my father, and me.

Dad is taller, so he spots it first. You couldn't see it from floor level because of the mountains of paper in the way. But from here, the high angle gives us a clear view. Drawn on the light cement wall in thick black magic marker are three neat swastikas.

The cameraman shakes his head. "I think the focus of our story just shifted a little."

CHAPTER NINETEEN

REELTOK

From the YouTube channel of Adam Tok

Interview with Sheriff Bennett Ocasek

REELTOK: Thanks, Sheriff, for taking time from your busy schedule to share your insights with TokNation.

SHERIFF OCASEK: Spare me. I think you're a loudmouth and a troublemaker. If it was up to me, you'd be run out of town on a rail.

REELTOK: Too bad that pesky First Amendment keeps getting in the way. Something about freedom of speech? So tell me, why are you here with me today?

SHERIFF OCASEK: Because I took a look at your fancy YouTube channel, and God knows why, but a lot of people tune in to hear what you've got to say.

REELTOK: Seventeen million subscribers and growing.

SHERIFF OCASEK: And I want them to know—and anybody else who might be listening—that we're good people here in Chokecherry. Yeah, we've got our cranks. Who doesn't? But anything that happened here in the past is exactly there—in the past.

REELTOK: So you're confirming the Night of a Thousand Flames.

SHERIFF OCASEK: Don't put words in my mouth. I'm not confirming anything. I'm not denying anything either. I was a kid back then.

REELTOK: But you can't deny the swastikas that are happening now, practically every day. What progress has your department made identifying who's responsible?

SHERIFF OCASEK: We're working on it.

REELTOK: *Are* you working on it? You don't seem to have much to show for your efforts after all these weeks.

SHERIFF OCASEK: There are six hundred kids in that school. You know how long it would take for one of them to pull a marker and scribble a few lines on a wall or a locker? I may not be some big-shot New Yorker, but I'm smart enough to know what you're implying. You think we haven't found the culprit because we're not really looking. We think it's fine to have swastikas all over the place because we're the same bunch of rednecks and racists we were in 1978.

REELTOK: Your words, not mine.

SHERIFF OCASEK: If it's racism you want, you should have a look at your own followers. Do you even read your comments section?

REELTOK: Are you kidding? TokNation are Chokecherry's biggest supporters. Where do you think that art supply company found out about your paper chain? Schools all over the country are working on their own chains to send here to help you get to six million!

SHERIFF OCASEK: I guess you don't read the ones that are not so nice. The lady who thinks it's so terrible to waste learning time cutting and gluing paper. And by the way, she wants to know what's so bad about swastikas? They're just little pictures. Or the guy who says it's a crime to waste forests of paper to commemorate something that "never happened."

REELTOK: Free speech applies to everybody, even people who are mixed up.

SHERIFF OCASEK: Just to be clear, that's the *Holocaust* he's talking about.

REELTOK: You've got cranks; I've got cranks.

SHERIFF OCASEK: Yeah, so this message is for your cranks. Leave us alone. If you think that swastikas are fine and the Holocaust never happened—you couldn't be more wrong. The hate shown here isn't just about people who are Jewish or Black or anything else. It's about us all—every single one of us! Hate is hate, and hate hurts everybody.

REELTOK: Well said, Sheriff. Bravo . . . and yet the swastikas continue.

SHERIFF OCASEK: If you don't like our swastikas, well, neither do we. We're not perfect, but let us work out our problems in our own way. And if you don't like our paper chain, I've got one word for you: tough.

CHAPTER TWENTY

DANA LEVINSON

Today, the paper chain hits one million links. The whole school goes nuts when Michael makes the announcement—but not for very long. We spend a couple of minutes cheering and then go right back to work making links. It's an amazing achievement, but we're still five times that many away from reaching our goal.

We'll never get there. I mean, it's obviously *possible*. As my scientist father puts it, "If you can do one million in a month and a half, you can do six million in nine months. The question is, can you get an entire town to do nothing but glue paper loops for nine solid months?"

It's even more complicated than that. Will more paper donations continue when our current supply runs out? Will the carloads and boxloads of links keep coming? Thanks to ReelTok, the whole country knows about our project. Art classes everywhere are sending us big boxes crammed with paper chain to add to ours. We've gotten shipments from as far away as California, Maryland, and even Canada.

I guess what I'm saying is I *believe* now. I know I had mixed feelings about the project at the beginning. As the Jewish girl, I took everything about it too personally. When it petered out, it would be because nobody thought *I* was worth the effort. But I don't own the Holocaust. Neither does Link—whose great-grandparents died in it. It's called a crime against humanity because all humans co-own the responsibility never to forget it.

To stand in the farm equipment warehouse, surrounded by a million links of paper chain, piled to the ceiling, is an emotional experience that's hard to describe. These aren't just paper links; they represent a million lost souls, and you're recognizing them in a physical way. Maybe it's who I am, but I get choked up just thinking about it.

One thing is certain: If we do get to six million—or even two million—we're going to need a bigger warehouse. The fire marshal says we can't fill this one up any more. Going forward, our paper chain will be stored in the Chokecherry Municipal Garage. They're moving all the snowplows and road graders outside to make room for our new production. All we have to do is keep it coming. Will we?

"It'll fizzle out eventually," Dad predicts. "Kids' attention spans are notoriously short. A new video game comes out; a royal baby gets born. A hit song, a dance craze. And people will drift to other things."

I can't even disagree with him. Chokecherry Middle School has done something incredible with the paper chain, but we're only human. Just the fact that the entire seventh grade is so obsessed with the Jordie-Pamela breakup is proof of that.

I honestly didn't even realize the two of them were together. Whenever I start to feel like the paper chain has brought the Wexford-Smythe kids into the mainstream, along comes something like this to prove we're still outsiders. Jordie and Pamela are an item? All I've ever seen them do is fight. I once overheard them arguing over which was the luckier number—five or three. You'd have thought the future of the planet depended on it. It sounded like a lot of things; romance wasn't any of them. And yet the same kids who have exceeded all expectations and gone above and beyond to pull off something as selfless and wonderful as the paper chain eagerly spend hours analyzing one pointless breakup that's happened ten times before and, anyway, is none of their business. Whose fault is it? Who did the actual dumping? Was it in person or by text? Why is Pamela hanging around Pouncey now? Will Jordie find another girl on the rebound? Will they make up, or is this the end? Andrew says some eighth graders are taking bets on when the famous couple will get back together. If it happens December 17, he wins eighty-five bucks.

By the way, if those two never get back together, the money will go toward fresh supplies for the paper chain. So that's what I'm rooting for. Call me anti-love.

"Hey, kid! Hey!"

Dad drives us to school in the morning, but he's out at the dig all day, so we have to walk home. I'm on my way to pick up Ryan at the elementary school when I hear someone calling me. A quick glance over my shoulder. It's that eighth grader, Erick Federov.

"Hey, you! Jewish girl!"

I wheel on him, and he adds, "Dana."

"I have to pick up my brother," I tell him.

He speeds up to me. "I'll walk with you."

I stare straight ahead. "You've got your gym back. What's the problem now?"

He's surprised, because he doesn't know I overheard him complaining that time. "I wanted to ask you—how come you turned Link Rowley Jewish?"

I speed up. "I didn't turn Link Rowley anything. Link Rowley *is* Jewish." I've come to terms with it. By birth, he's every bit as Jewish as I am.

"No, he isn't. His family puts up Christmas lights. At least they did until you turned them. You're trying to turn the whole town Jewish with your paper chain!"

I stop in my tracks and turn to face him, even though he's a basketball player and eight inches taller than I am. "It's not *my* paper chain. I'm not even the person who came up with it."

"It's about the Holocaust, and that's a Jewish thing!"

Heat rushes into my cheeks. "You know what's a Jewish thing? Dealing with *idiots* who make comments like that one! First off, at least five million *non*-Jews also died in the Holocaust. Second, just imagine for a second a government deciding to wipe out every single person who was born into *your* religion. There's a word for that—*genocide*! And it's everybody's problem, because if it happens to one group, it can happen to *any* group. That's why the paper chain is for all of us—even you! It started with the school, but now it belongs to everybody.

Don't you watch ReelTok? The whole country's in on it now!" I wheel and storm away. This time he doesn't follow me.

Seeing Ryan calms me down a little. He runs out the door to meet me, proudly waving a section of paper chain five links long and two-thirds crushed. "Look what I made in art!"

"That's great," I tell him. "I'll take it to school tomorrow to add to the big chain."

"Do you think it'll get us to two million?" he asks.

Ryan is obsessed with the numbers. He's always talking about how many links we have: how many thousands, tens of thousands, hundreds of thousands. Now that we've hit a million, he expects to make it to two million any day now, since two is only one more than one.

"This will definitely help," I assure him, and he's pleased to bits.

At home, we find Link on the porch swing, buried in his papers from Rabbi Gold, chanting quietly under his breath.

Ryan corrects his pronunciation of a couple of Hebrew words.

"Thanks." Link makes notes on the page. "Dana, your kid brother's really smart."

Tell me about it. Ryan has already memorized Link's entire temple service just from listening to Rabbi Gold's recording so many times. He's not the only one. I swear I heard Michael humming one of the blessings under his breath as he counted up paper chain links a couple of days ago.

I let the three of us into the house. Ryan heads to his room, and Link and I hit the bar mitzvah books. Link can handle most of it on his own now, so I work on my homework. Not sure why he needs me anymore—I'm really just a safety net in case he has a question.

He's still here when Mom gets home, so she invites him to stay for dinner.

"Thanks, Dr. Levinson. It's good to meet you."

"We've met," she assures him.

He frowns. "Really?"

Her brow clouds. "You might not remember. You were busy at the time."

"Vacuuming the fertilizer out of the office," I supply when Link seems totally bewildered.

Ryan cackles. "Did it stink?"

"Kind of," Link admits sheepishly.

I'm half rooting for him to be too embarrassed to stick around to face my father after that. But he does, and the five of us sit down around the kitchen table.

He takes a tiny bite of his taco and chews as if he's afraid the stuff is radioactive.

"Is something wrong?" Dad asks him finally.

Link swallows gingerly. "Is this kosher?"

Mom stares at him. "You're *kosher* now too?"

"It's a taco!" I explode. "It has meat and cheese. It can't be kosher."

"We don't keep kosher," my father informs him. "I actually don't think it would be possible to find kosher food in Chokecherry."

"Sorry," Link mumbles, shamefaced.

"Link, chill out," I say. "You don't have to apologize on behalf of the town. Not everything's about racism, you know. They don't sell kosher food here because there'd be no one to buy it. Not even us."

"It's not that." His face is flushed. "I mean—the fertilizer in the mail slot. It was supposed to be dinosaur poop."

Ryan snickers. "Link said *poop* at the table."

"We get the joke," my mother tells Link. "It was my husband who first identified the fossilized stegosaur droppings for the university."

"It was a stupid thing to do," Link goes on in a tortured voice. "I don't know what I was thinking. I did a lot of stupid things back then . . ."

His voice trails off, leaving him staring into his plate. It's pretty awkward.

Dad breaks the uncomfortable silence. "That's all in the past. Now you've set yourself a positive goal and you're working toward it. You're on the right path."

I stare at my father. How can a bar mitzvah be the right path for this kid who grew up going to church, hunting Easter eggs, and writing letters to Santa?

And yet, for the very first time since Link approached me in the cafeteria, I can sort of picture it.

CHAPTER TWENTY-ONE

REELTOK

From the YouTube channel of Adam Tok

Interview with Michael Amorosa

> **REELTOK:** I'm pleased to welcome Michael Amorosa, art director of the Chokecherry Middle School's paper chain project.
>
> **MICHAEL:** Sorry, can't talk now. UPS just delivered a stack of new boxes full of paper chain for me to check in.
>
> **REELTOK:** Thirty-four new boxes, to be exact.
>
> **MICHAEL:** How would you know that?
>
> **REELTOK:** TokNation has members everywhere, including at UPS.
>
> **MICHAEL:** We've had packages from over forty states, and countries all around the world. We're closing in on two million links!
>
> **REELTOK:** You're welcome.
>
> **MICHAEL:** Don't you get it? One person has to keep track of all that: me!

REELTOK: What's it like to count two million paper links?

MICHAEL: Well, I can't count every single one. I just keep a running total—you know, three hundred here, five hundred there, two thousand in a carton.

REELTOK: And how do you verify the numbers are correct?

MICHAEL: By length. We know the average link takes up about four inches, so if the count is off, we'll catch it. We've already filled up the farm equipment warehouse and the Chokecherry Municipal Garage. We've started on the abandoned silo at the Beaverton farm. And a lot of people have volunteered their spare rooms, basements, and attics. The whole town is on board.

REELTOK: Well, there has to be at least one person who isn't on board. The swastikas are still coming, right? You found the first one. Do you have any idea who might be doing it?

MICHAEL: I—I—I gotta go.

CHAPTER TWENTY-TWO

JORDIE DUROS

If Pam thinks I'm going to come crawling back to her over broken glass, then she's losing what's left of her mind.

Just because we got back together all those other times doesn't mean things are always going to go that way. We're done. Through. Finished. Finito.

This isn't like when we broke up because she likes her peanut-butter-and-jelly sandwiches on wheat bread, when everybody knows white bread is the only bread for a PBJ. That was babyish. You don't throw away a relationship that's been going on since second grade over a sandwich, no matter how wrongheaded the other person is being.

It isn't even like the time when she told me to buy the sneakers with the four stripes and I accidentally bought the sneakers with the three stripes, but it was too late to take them back, because I'd already stepped in gum.

This is different. Pam and I have a thing where we always see every Marvel movie the first Saturday it's in theaters. Sometimes Link, Pouncey, and Sophie come with us, but for sure, the two of us never miss. Anyway, the new one is coming out the weekend of December 4, and Pam wants me to buy advance tickets—there's only one theater in Chokecherry, and when it sells out, that's it. So I told her December 4 is no good, because we're both going to be in Shadbush Crossing that day for Link's bar mitzvah.

She looked at me like I had a cabbage for a head. "I'm not going to any dumb bar mitzvah! I'm not Jewish and neither is Link!"

So I said, "I don't really understand it either. But if Link thinks this is important, that's good enough for me." Then, to show her how reasonable I am, I added, "Why don't we go to the movie on December fifth?"

You would have thought I suggested we hunt down Captain America himself and gut him like a trout. She went off on me. December 5 is her dance recital—like I'm supposed to memorize her schedule! "If you're such a bar mitzvah lover," she snapped, "why don't you go with Dana?"

That really confused me. I barely said three words to Dana before the paper chain project, and even now I wouldn't describe us as friends. Then it dawned on me what she meant. A bar mitzvah is a Jewish thing, and Dana is Jewish.

And I got mad, because that was kind of mean. So I said something mean back. I told her she dances like a spider on a hot plate, and if I want to see that, all I have to do is turn on the barbecue after a long winter.

Piece of friendly advice: Never insult your girlfriend's dancing. They're sensitive about that.

So not only am I a single man again, but now I'm probably

going to break my perfect record of seeing every Marvel movie all the way back to *Thor: Ragnarok.*

"You guys'll make up," Link assures me. "You always do."

"I don't know, man. She gave me back my Iron Man bracelet. She's never done that before. I was a real jerk this time."

Sophie volunteers to talk to her and comes back looking grim. "I'll give it another week and try again."

Pouncey tries to put in a good word for me, but his only report is "You really blew it this time, Einstein."

Leave it to Pouncey, who's wrong about everything, to be right about this.

The thing is, the more I act like I don't care, the more it bugs me. It would be easier if I could just move to Venezuela or something, but I have to see her every day at school. We're in the same homeroom and have the same lunch hour. She picks a different lab partner in science, so I have to work with Caroline, who talks my ear off. When we're paper-chaining, Pam makes sure to set up on the opposite side of whatever room we're in. And no matter who's with her over there, she smiles and laughs and acts like she's having a way better time than she'd be having if she was with loser me.

It stinks. But you know what? She really does dance like a spider on a hot plate.

When I walked through the school halls, kids used to look at me with admiration and respect. Now they just shake their heads in sympathy. I keep expecting to feel better, but every day it's a little worse.

I have an orthodontist appointment on Wednesday, so I get to school late. I'm heading down the back hall to first period when I spot Pam running in the opposite direction. I've seen her a million times since we split, but this is my first chance to talk to her with nobody else around. And I've already decided that I'm going to make up with her no matter what. That's how it always goes with Pam and me. One of us has to swallow our pride and take the blame for the whole breakup. It has nothing to do with who's wrong and who's right. It's just my turn.

I wave. "Pam—over here!"

As she pounds down the hall in my direction, she definitely doesn't seem happy to see me. I try to read her expression. Angry? Sad?

I plow ahead. "I didn't mean what I said about your dancing. You dance great—"

That's when it hits me—she's not slowing down.

I give it one more try. I step directly into her path. "Pam, please listen—"

She reaches out a hand and shoves me away so hard that I stagger back and land on my butt. She doesn't even turn around to see if she's killed me. By the time I scramble to my feet, she's disappeared around the corner.

So that's it. We're through for good. Pouncey said it all: I really blew it this time.

I feel like going home, crawling into bed, and binge-watching

Netflix on my phone for three straight weeks. But I don't. I have to get on with my life eventually. I might as well start now.

Link tells me, "Sorry, man." And he means it. But the very next minute he's mumbling in Hebrew, humming that tuneless tune, and forgetting he's got a friend who's suffering. The old Link wouldn't say sorry. He'd come up with an epic prank—something hilarious to distract us and make us laugh. But these days, it's all bar mitzvah, all the time. When you need support, some guy singing in a foreign language is a lousy substitute. And since he's off the soccer team, the sports connection between us is gone too. That leaves just Pouncey, who is zero comfort. You don't go to Pouncey for sympathy. Pouncey's the guy you feel sympathy *for*.

And it doesn't help that the whole school is tense and on edge. The word is that a new swastika was discovered this morning. You'd think we'd have gotten used to it by now, but we never do. It's always awful. The teachers freak out and start being mean to the kids, like six hundred of us got together to hold the paintbrush. We get weird because we're feeling guilty for something we didn't even do—all but one of us anyway. It's the poison icing on the lousy cake.

So surely I'm at rock bottom, right? It can't get any worse.

Wrong. In Spanish, I can't figure out why Señora Wallace keeps staring at me. Maybe I'm imagining things—a day like today would make anybody paranoid. But at the end of the period, she pulls me aside.

"Jordan, your shirt—"

"It's a West Ham United jersey," I explain. "My favorite English soccer club."

"Yes, but—" She points to a spot on my chest. "That stain. Where did you get it?"

"Stain?" I look down. It's hard to see against the wine-colored fabric of the jersey, but there's a light purple splotch about the size of my fist just below the team crest. "My mom's going to kill me. You don't know what she went through to get this shirt."

"But where did it come from?" she persists.

"We had to order it from London."

"No, I mean the *stain*."

I shrug. "I was at the orthodontist this morning. Maybe something dripped on me. You know, fluoride, disinfectant, toothpaste—"

"Come with me," she interrupts. "We're going to the principal."

I'm stunned. "What did I do?"

"Let's just see what Mr. Brademas says."

As I follow her through the school, I'm completely blown away. Am I in trouble for having a dirty shirt? Since when is bad cleanliness against the rules? Pouncey spends half his life covered in food, and he never gets dragged to the principal's office. Is this a new thing starting today?

Señora Wallace doesn't even drop me off, but walks me right into the inner office while the secretary pages Mr. Brademas. If the school has suddenly decided to get tough on stains, why did they have to pick me to make an example of?

Lost in my swirling thoughts, I glance through the glass wall of the office and spy Mr. Kennedy and one of the other custodians cleaning the glass of the main floor trophy case. It was always a special place for me because I'm an athlete, so I was on the teams that won a lot of those awards. But now all I can think of is that this must be where the latest swastika was drawn. It's not there anymore, but the custodians are scrubbing at what's left of it, their sponges dripping purple paint.

Light purple paint, almost exactly the color of . . .

Mr. Brademas hits the office running, and I instantly understand why. He isn't sprinting to enforce a new cleanliness code. He thinks he's caught the swastika guy and it's *me*!

I leap to my feet, sputtering like a car with a bad engine. "But—it's not me! It can't be! I checked in late. Ask anybody!"

"That's true," the secretary calls in through the office door. "I have the slip here. It's marked nine thirty-seven."

The principal is undaunted. "Where did you get that paint on your shirt?"

"I don't know!" I babble. My fluoride theory is pretty much out the window. What are the odds that my orthodontist uses fluoride the same color as the latest swastika? "I must have bumped into something!"

Mr. Brademas is like one of those TV cops in the interrogation cell. "Tell me everything you did from the moment you walked into the building."

"Well, I missed homeroom. I was late to math, and I went to Spanish. Then Señora brought me here."

"I want every detail," he insists. "Don't leave anything out. Everything you did. Everyone you met."

"I didn't talk to anybody," I say honestly. "I ran into Pamela Bynes in the back hall, but she was running too fast to—"

I relive the moment in a flash. I step into her path. She pushes me out of the way. I feel the shove—*in exactly the spot of the stain on my jersey.*

Mr. Brademas is already instructing the secretary to page Pam out of class.

"But it can't be Pam," I tell him. "She would never do anything like that."

The principal is grim. "I just want to ask her where she got the paint on her hand that she transferred to your shirt."

"Maybe she brushed against the trophy case," I suggest hopefully.

"Maybe." He doesn't sound convinced.

The principal takes me to Pam's locker, number 318. Mr. Kennedy is already there. Pam arrives, accompanied by Coach Ventnor, the girls' PE teacher.

"Pamela, please open your locker for inspection," Mr. Brademas orders.

"I don't have to," she says in a shaky voice. "It's an invasion of my privacy."

I shoot her an encouraging smile. Why make a big deal out of this? She has nothing to hide.

The look on her face is absolute panic. That's the first inkling I get that she *does* have something to hide. Something huge.

In a strangely kind voice, the principal says, "Please don't make this any more unpleasant than it already has to be."

When Pam doesn't answer, he nods to Mr. Kennedy. The custodian takes a large metal clipper from his tool belt and prepares to cut the lock.

"Stop!" I blurt. And when they turn to me, it all comes pouring out. Even though she hates me now, I have to protect her if I can. "You don't have to open the locker. I'm the swastika guy, not Pam."

Pam's eyes widen in surprise and something like relief.

Mr. Brademas frowns. "You just explained to me that you were at an orthodontist appointment."

"I lied," I say readily. "And I forged a fake late slip."

The principal doesn't reply. Instead he nods to his custodian. The lock comes away with a snap and the door swings wide.

Mr. Brademas reaches inside and pulls out a small paint can and a two-inch brush, bristles still wet.

The color on the label reads: *Lilac/Purple*.

CHAPTER TWENTY-THREE

DANA LEVINSON

The rumors start around lunchtime.

I already sense that the level of buzzing energy in the cafeteria is higher than usual, but I first hear the news when Andrew approaches me in the food line.

"They caught him."

"Caught who?" I ask.

"The swastika guy! Brademas busted him this morning. Didn't you see the cop cars outside?"

I don't know why I'm so shocked. When the first few swastikas were appearing, I definitely expected the culprit to be found out at some point. But when that didn't happen, I suppose I sort of got used to them and figured they'd go on forever. Like our vandal was some kind of swastika supervillain who was too smart and wily ever to be tripped up.

"Who is it?" I ask.

He shrugs, rattling the plastic cutlery on his tray. "Nobody knows. But they can't keep it a secret forever."

At our table, all the talk is about the identity of the mysterious racist/vandal/jerk.

"It's Christopher Solis," Caroline says positively. "It has to be. I just saw him ten minutes ago. They've got him in in-school suspension."

"That kid lives in in-school suspension," Michael counters. "I doubt he's spent two hours out of it all year. Besides, it can't be him. The cops took away whoever did it."

I've been staying out of the blame game so far, but as I set down my tray opposite Michael, a thought occurs to me. "How about Erick Federov? He said some weird things to me a few days ago. And not weird-strange. Weird-*awful*."

Andrew shakes his head. "Uh-uh. The eighth-grade jocks were at the high school all morning, working out with the JV soccer team."

"Are we a hundred percent positive it wasn't an adult?" Michael asks.

"It's not Mr. Kennedy," I assure him. "Get that idea out of your head. He's eating lunch on the bench out front, so he's definitely not under arrest."

Caroline looks worried. "Now that the swastikas are over, I sure hope people don't lose interest in the paper chain."

Michael rolls his eyes. "Don't I wish. At this point, I'm getting black lung disease from inhaling too many construction paper molecules."

At that moment, Pouncey steps out of the food line, juggling a heavily laden tray. An audible groan goes up in the cafeteria. A lot of kids probably had him pegged as suspect number one for the swastikas. Seeing him in school instead of in custody means it's time to go back to the drawing board. He crosses the lunchroom and sits down with Link and Jordie.

"Another theory down the drain," Michael comments. "And I heard Jordie got dragged to the principal's office this morning, but that must have been about something else."

I can't help noticing that Link's bar mitzvah folder is closed, and he, Jordie, and Pouncey are having an intense conversation. Not even the popular kids are immune to today's swastika gossip. In a small town like Chokecherry, it's just too juicy.

I get my first whiff of the answer in science. Eli is whining to the teacher that his lab partner stood him up, so he's missing half the prep work for the experiment. Who's his lab partner? Pamela Bynes.

That confuses me, because Pamela always worked with Jordie. But of course that had to change when those two broke up. I glance over at Jordie. He looks stricken, his face paper white.

"Pamela Bynes isn't in school," I whisper to Michael in the hall after class. "She was helping with the paper chain this morning, but now she's gone."

He nods. "I heard. Everybody's talking about it. And the lock is missing from her locker."

As the day goes on, the name Pamela bubbles out of every conversation, spoken quietly, but so often that it's a growing echo in the school. There's no announcement from the office, and several times I overhear teachers saying things like "I can't give out that kind of information about a student," and "I'm sorry, that's confidential," and even "Mind your own business, please."

It just makes the rumors louder and wilder, and always with Pamela at the center. She's the prime suspect, the only suspect.

Pamela? Really? I wouldn't have guessed her in a million

years. Not that she's my best friend or anything like that. She's part of Link's crowd. I always think of her and Sophie as practically twins. A little shallow and self-centered, maybe. But *this*?

If Pamela is a white supremacist, she's done a pretty good job hiding it. She's never said anything out of line to me, and I haven't heard of anyone like Michael or Andrew having a problem with her. Stranger still, she was one of the very first volunteers to work on the paper chain. That's our way of fighting *against* the swastikas. Why would she join that effort if she's on the other side? The more I think about it, the less sense it makes.

I have a giddy flashback to the very first paper-chaining day in the art room. Pamela and Jordie had a fight, and she ran out. Immediately after that, a new swastika was discovered. And she was working at the warehouse when the swastikas appeared there. If Pamela really is the culprit, the evidence was right in front of us, and nobody twigged to it.

My head is spinning with the effort of trying to connect the dots on this. I'm not the only one. Every class change, the babble of speculation in the halls gets a little bit louder, and the teachers look a little bit more desperate.

After school, the volunteer turnout for paper-chaining is the smallest it's been since the beginning of the project. Pamela is all anyone can talk about. Can this popular girl most of them have known since kindergarten be the dreaded swastika guy?

I'm dying to know, but there's nobody to ask. The other kids are going on pure rumor, same as me. I'm on my way to pick up Ryan when it comes to me: Who always knows more about Chokecherry's swastika problems than anybody in town?

When I open the YouTube app on my phone, it takes me straight to Adam Tok's channel. I'm not a fan—I think the guy is an obnoxious loudmouth. But it's hard to resist when that mouth is speaking about your own school.

The top video is titled "FINALLY!!!" And when I tap it, the famous unibrow is crammed into the frame of my phone screen. "Cheerleader!" he barks. "Athlete! All-American girl!" The blogger's face is replaced by a montage of pictures of Pamela, beginning with her as a pigtailed preschooler and ending with a photo of the Chokecherry Middle School cheer squad, her face circled in red. "A small-town sweetheart with a deep, dark secret called racism."

So it's true. I never realized how much I was hoping against it. It would have been better if it had turned out to be a stranger—a sixth or eighth grader I didn't see in homeroom every day. I know Pamela and she knows me. Somehow that makes everything more personal.

"The mystery of the swastikas has been solved, TokNation!" ReelTok rants on. "Pamela Ann Bynes, a seventh grader at Chokecherry Middle School, is the architect of all that vandalism and all that hate. Students are shocked. Teachers are dismayed. A community reels in disbelief. 'How could this happen in our tiny perfect town?' The answer: Maybe your tiny town was never as perfect as you thought it was . . ."

"Dana, wait!" Link is jogging toward me. "I can't make it today. Something came up."

"Something sure did," I agree, brandishing my phone. "Did you know about any of this?"

He shakes his head. "Neither did Jordie, and he was closer to her than anybody."

ReelTok is still raving. "Chokecherry may deny its scandalous past, but you can't paint over rot. It's still there, TokNation, and it will always come out." The screen shows an old black-and-white photograph of a Klansman in full regalia, his hood cradled in his right arm, gazing proudly into the camera. "Meet Elvin Roy Bynes, great-uncle to Pamela, and head of the Shadbush County chapter of the KKK. He died in 2014, but wouldn't he be proud to see little Pamela following in his footsteps?"

Link whistles. "I knew about Pouncey's grandfather, but this is the first I'm hearing about Pamela's family. I mean, she always said the newspapers made up the Night of a Thousand Flames, but—"

I cut him off. "That's horrible! Denying the past is the surest way to make sure it happens again! It *did* happen again, sort of. What do you think all those swastikas mean? And *she's* the one who drew them!"

He regards me closely. "Are you okay?"

I shake my head. "It's just different when it turns out to be someone you know."

He looks uncomfortable. "Yeah, I hear you. See you tomorrow."

As I watch Link jog off, I spy a crowd gathering in the park across from the middle school. ReelTok's park—a large group of kids lining up to be interviewed. I can imagine what they're going to say: *I knew it all along! There was always something rotten about Pamela Bynes! She stole my spot on the track team! She beat me out on the cheerleading squad! She broke Jordie's heart! She took the last Twinkie after I called dibs! Of course she did the swastikas!*

I'm furious at Pamela. What she did was awful, unforgivable. But in a strange way, I feel bad for her too. Her name is mud not just around here, but thanks to ReelTok, all over the world. Kids are lining up to denounce her. She's probably going to be expelled from school. She's in trouble with the law, and might even end up in juvie. And for what? How could what she did possibly be so important to her?

I want to scream at her. In anger, yeah, but also to ask: What were you thinking? Was it worth it to mess up your whole life for the sake of a few dozen lines scrawled on walls and lockers and garbage dumpsters? Is it really that important to make people like me and Michael and Andrew and, yeah, Link uncomfortable? Do you think your late great-uncle is celebrating you somewhere?

What Pamela did was hateful, but what's even harder to take is how *pointless* it was. There's no question that she did damage to the town by exposing raw nerves and bringing up the sins of Chokecherry's past. But that's balanced out by the *good* things that came in reaction to the swastikas—like the paper chain and Link learning the truth about his heritage. Mostly, the damage she did was to herself.

What a waste.

ReelTok is still ranting through the speaker of my phone, outlining the history of Elvin Roy Bynes and the Shadbush County chapter of the Klan. The vlogger may be a jerk, but you can't say anything about his reporting skills. Pamela has barely been arrested, yet he already has her entire family history cued up and all set to go. I turn it off when the elementary school comes into view. No need for Ryan to hear this. Obviously, he knows about the swastikas, but he doesn't really grasp what they mean. To him, they're mostly the spark that inspired our paper chain—and isn't it great?

How did ReelTok do all that research on Pamela while sitting in a park? Oh, sure, he has a laptop with him, but that doesn't explain everything. He has pictures. Details nobody else found. He's posted—I check—*six* videos in the past hour and a half! Not even the most celebrated journalist of all time could accomplish all that. Unless—

What if he already knew that Pamela was guilty? And instead of telling anyone, he did his research in advance and waited for her to get caught. And there he was, locked and loaded, ready to splash the story all over YouTube the minute the truth came out.

Of course! What other explanation could there be? We thought it was plain old cussedness that kept him in that park, day after day, rain or shine. But he wasn't just doing it to be stubborn and thumb his nose at the town. He was *spying* on the school. And he must have seen Pamela where she had no business being and put two and two together.

He knew all along! He could have put a stop to this misery weeks ago, but instead he chose not to. Why?

To attract more followers to his YouTube channel.

I always knew ReelTok was sleazy, but this is a whole new level of sleaze. He came to town acting like our mouthpiece, here to tell our story to the world. And he did. Thanks to his global audience, thousands of paper chains are arriving at school every day. For sure, we never could have reached nearly three million links without the publicity he gave us.

But for a guy who claims to be helping Chokecherry, he seems to hate the place. He never misses a chance to call us small-minded hicks and he's always reminding his TokNation about the town's racist history, hinting that those days aren't as far in the past as we'd like everybody to believe.

He's manipulating us. And we're letting him.

That brings up a bigger question: If he already knew about Pamela, what else does he know?

CHAPTER TWENTY-FOUR

REELTOK

From the YouTube channel of Adam Tok

Interview with Jordie Duros

REELTOK: The word is that you and Pamela Bynes are going out. Is it true?

JORDIE: It's complicated.

REELTOK: TokNation loves complicated. Tell us about it.

JORDIE: We've always had a kind of on-again, off-again thing. Right now, it's off again.

REELTOK: Did you break up with Pamela because she turned out to be behind the swastikas?

JORDIE: Actually, she broke up with me. And it happened before anybody found out about—you know. There's this new Marvel movie—it's a long story. Do you really need to hear about my personal life?

REELTOK: And before the breakup, you had no idea that your girlfriend was painting swastikas all over the school?

JORDIE: Of course not! Pam's not like that!

REELTOK: But now we know she *is* like that.

JORDIE: I—I guess we do.

REELTOK: And how does that make you feel?

JORDIE: How do you think it makes me feel? This is someone I've been close to my whole life. Now there's this, like, dark side to her I had no clue even existed. And every time we broke up, we always got back together. But this time—I don't know.

REELTOK: Have you spoken with her since she was arrested?

JORDIE: Her folks won't let her talk to anyone. It's all so messed up. Anyway, at least the swastika thing is over.

REELTOK: Well, it's not *really* over, is it?

JORDIE: What do you mean? Pam's kicked out of school. She's under house arrest. Word is her family's thinking about moving out of Chokecherry. You think she's going to do more swastikas now?

REELTOK: You mean you haven't heard?

JORDIE: Heard what?

REELTOK: Pamela admits to all the swastikas except one—the first one. She claims the original swastika in the atrium of the school was someone else's work. She's a copycat, not the original.

JORDIE: Why would you believe her, knowing what she did?

REELTOK: Why would she lie about that one when she's confessing to all the others? It's not like she'd be in less trouble for twenty-six swastikas than twenty-seven. She even kept track of the number. But I've seen the police report. TokNation has members in all sorts of places. She's absolutely adamant that the first one, the one in the atrium, was put there by somebody else.

JORDIE: But that means—

REELTOK: You've caught one white supremacist, but there's another one still out there. This mystery is far from over.

CHAPTER TWENTY-FIVE

MICHAEL AMOROSA

I'm standing atop the scaffolding at the abandoned silo at the Beaverton farm, feeding an endless chain of paper links through the intake window. If you want to know what eight hundred thousand links look like, picture a forty-foot silo attached to a small barn. When the first chains went in, we figured we'd never fill it up. Scratch that. It's multicolored paper to the roof.

"Stop the lift!" I call down to Pouncey, who's working the hand crank that keeps bucket after bucket of chain rising up the rounded side of the silo and spilling in through the opening.

He doesn't hear me over the screeching of the rusted mechanism. All around him, kids stagger under massive armloads of chain, waiting to be loaded. It'll never fit inside the silo. We'll have to take it to the Vardis' basement, our next designated storage space.

"Stop!" I shout a little louder. "We're all full up here!"

Pouncey keeps on cranking. At the top, I'm stuffing as hard as I can, while yelling, "Stop! Stop! Stop!"

Link glances briefly up at me, before returning his attention to his bar mitzvah folder.

A low rumbling comes from beneath me, and the whole silo begins to vibrate. At the base of the structure, thrusters fire, throwing Pouncey, Link, and the others clear of the barn.

"What's happening?" I bellow at the top of my lungs.

As the silo begins to rise with a fearsome roar, I hang on to the scaffolding for dear life. Eight hundred thousand paper links have turned the overstuffed structure into a rocket. I flatten myself to the wooden platform as the fiery engines fly past me and pray I won't be vaporized.

On the ground, kids are gazing up, pointing and cheering, as the silo heads out of the atmosphere.

"Look!" Caroline shrieks joyfully. "We're going to have student government on the moon!"

I struggle to my feet and watch as the rocket grows smaller and smaller and finally winks out of sight in the stratosphere. All I can think of is eight hundred thousand links lost.

Oh man, I counted eight hundred thousand links for nothing.

"Michael!" My mother is shaking me by the shoulder. "Wake up! You're having a bad dream. There's no rocket."

I roll over in bed, blinking. "Sorry, sorry. I'll go back to sleep."

"Well, no, you can't," she tells me. "It's time to get up for school."

In a normal year, I'd be begging and pleading to go in late with a note of excuse. But this year, the school will be packed with volunteers starting at seven a.m. They'll be making paper chains—and no one will be there to count them. By eight o'clock, the deliveries will start arriving—chains from all over the country and all around the globe. Now that our project has gotten famous, FedEx and UPS are delivering paper links from other schools for free. It's an avalanche.

My current tally of links stands at 4,326,718, stored in warehouses, silos, basements, and attics around town. Mr. Brademas was wrong. It isn't impossible to get to six million links. With the world's help, it's practically a slam dunk.

So I drag myself out of bed, throw on some clothes, and present myself in the kitchen. My mother places in front of me a plate with four fried eggs, hash browns, and a pretty big piece of steak.

"What's this?" I ask.

"Breakfast."

"For who?" I demand. "The Marine Corps?"

"You've lost weight," she accuses. "It's because of the paper chain."

"The paper chain is the best thing that's ever happened to Chokecherry," I argue. "The whole world is helping us. And now that the swastikas are a thing of the past, there's no downside anymore. It's a win-win for everybody."

Some detective I turned out to be. Pamela Bynes—wow. One of our very first paper-chaining volunteers! And now we're supposed to believe that she didn't paint the first one.

Why should we listen to someone rotten enough to do what Pamela did? On the other hand, why would she lie? It's not like doing one less swastika means she's in any less trouble.

Just thinking about it makes my head hurt. I'm pretty sure the other minority kids are sweating that too. We have no choice but to take all this a little more seriously than everybody else.

"Your health is more important than any paper chain," Mom lectures. "You're not getting enough rest, and you're having bad dreams. Do you know you count in your sleep? And I know it isn't sheep. No one counts four million sheep."

We argue over how much breakfast I should eat, compromising at two eggs and some of the steak. She puts the rest in Tupperware for my "after-school snack." I agree only because there's a zero percent chance I'll make it home before dinner. These days, the paper chain has gone far beyond just ReelTok. Caroline and I have interviews with radio and TV stations, and newspapers and podcasts are interested too.

The other kid the media's interested in is Link. As our paper chain gets more and more attention, the word also spreads about the Chokecherry kid who is racing toward an unlikely bar mitzvah on December 4.

Word of our project is even reaching real Holocaust survivors. They're old now, and their numbers are dwindling. Some were in the concentration camps, others were hidden and protected by non-Jewish families—like what those French nuns did for Link's grandma. Most of them were our age and younger during the war. They lost everything and everybody. And even after the fall of the Third Reich, they spent years as refugees.

That morning, after an hour of paper-chaining, we pack in front of the Smart Board in the library and Zoom with a group of survivors at a Jewish Community Center in Florida. Their stories are so terrible, so heartbreaking, that you want to run out of the library rather than have to listen to another word.

But nobody moves. As hard as it is, we all understand that what we're seeing is super important.

"I was pulled from the line because I had delicate fingers, which the guards said would be useful in the factory, loading ammunition belts. That was the last time I saw my family alive. I was eleven years old . . ."

"My parents left our village in Poland when we heard the Germans were coming. We sheltered in Russia, but there was no food. My father said, 'What can the Germans do to us that's worse than this?' So we went home, and when we got to our village, it was empty. Every man, woman, and child died in the camps . . ."

"I was a wrestler. I used to dream of using my strength to fight the Nazis. But they made me a Sonderkommando—it was my job to bring bodies from the gas chambers to the ovens for cremation. Every night, in my dreams, I am still doing this very thing . . ."

"My sister died of malnutrition at the camp at Terezín, near Prague. Left to starve, like so many others . . ."

"I used to pray every night that I would see my father again. But when I did, he was just loose skin over a skeleton, and his eyes were sunken and blank. When I tried to hug him, he shrank from me, and I knew then that he didn't recognize me . . ."

"My mother was alive when the Americans liberated our camp. But when she learned that all my brothers and sisters were gone, within a week, she was dead of grief . . ."

Every single one of us is in tears at this point. Nobody even tries to hide it. The stories go on and on. Each one is a tragedy by itself. I try to multiply them by six million. It's more than my brain can compute.

The incredible part is that these people, who have suffered so greatly and been through so much, are *fans*.

"We just want you young people to know how much we admire what you're doing," says one elderly lady with a European accent.

"*You* admire *us*?" Caroline sniffles. "What we're doing is nothing compared with what you lived through."

"Twenty years from now, none of us will be here to speak for ourselves," says another member of the Florida group, an old man leaning on a walker. "Your paper chain and your willingness to pass our stories on will be our voice going forward. Humanity can never be allowed to forget what happened."

That's something we've been hearing about the paper chain more and more often—the importance of *remembering*. At first, it made no sense to me. How could anyone ever forget something so enormous? But look at the Night of a Thousand Flames. That was a lot more recent than the Holocaust, and already half the people in Chokecherry claim it never happened.

The first woman speaks up again. "Is Lincoln Rowley there, by any chance?"

Cautiously, Link half rises from his chair and holds up one finger. "I'm right here."

"I look at you, and I see what could have been from my own family," she tells him. "Mazel tov on your bar mitzvah, young man. You honor us all by what you're doing."

And then the assembled old-timers give Link a round

of applause. Link sits back down, blushing bright red and blinking.

The man with the walker speaks again. "May I ask one favor?"

Without even thinking, I blurt, "Yes! Of course! Anything!" It makes no sense—what "favor" can a bunch of Colorado kids possibly do that could have any value to the survivors of such an atrocity? But we all know we have to try.

"It would mean a lot to me," the man goes on, "if you could write my mother's name on one of the links of your chain. She was"—he straightens, standing taller—"she *is* one of the six million you memorialize."

It's like the spark that ignites a brushfire. Suddenly, the Smart Board audio crackles with voices as the Florida group calls out names of lost loved ones and friends.

I stand up and wave my arms. "We will. Of course we will. If you give us the names, we'll make sure every one gets on a link."

It takes some doing. The European names are unfamiliar and hard to spell. Dana, Caroline, and I set up shop by the Smart Board, painstakingly listing parents and siblings, relatives and friends. We agonize over every vowel and consonant. We won't be graded on this, obviously. But it seems vital to get it right.

Next stop is the art room, where we divvy up these forty-two precious names and transfer them onto strips of colored paper, to be formed into loops and added to the chain. Our crew has never been so silent and solemn.

I look over at Link, working next to me. Besides the four

names assigned to him, he has two more strips. On them, he's written *Great-Grandma* and *Great-Grandpa*.

"My grandmother's parents," he explains to me. "Nobody knows their names, not even her."

I collect the links, but when I get to Jordie, his are still blank. He's hunched over in his chair, staring at his list like the names are giving him a stomachache.

"Take your time," I advise him gently. "Some of that spelling is next to impossible."

He looks at me, his eyes bleak with misery. Then he gets up and storms out into the hall.

I hesitate. I should probably see what's bugging him. But is it really any of my business? Besides paper-chaining, I don't have much to do with the popular kids. Maybe I should send Link or Sophie out there. But I don't "send" the popular kids either. President of the art club is not a position of authority.

I scan the room. Everybody's busy. Everybody except me.

In the hall, I find Jordie just outside the art room door, his face pressed against the tiles.

"How can I help?" I ask.

"I saw Pam last night," he tells me. "Her parents finally let me stop over."

"Oh, wow," I say. "I guess she feels pretty awful right now."

"That's just it." He turns to me, and I can see the outline of the bricks etched into his skin. "She thinks what she did was just fine and the only downside was getting caught. And then her dad told me that the town is crazy to make such a big deal out of nothing."

I let out my breath and realize I've been holding it. Since the news broke, I'll bet every kid in school has been wondering why Pamela did all those swastikas. Is she a vandal? A sick joker? A defacer of public property?

Now I have my answer. It's something worse than all those bad things. Hate, pure and simple. No do-overs, no excuses— except maybe the fact that she comes from a family that's even worse than she is.

"When we were on Zoom with the survivors," Jordie goes on, "I was like: 'Pam should be here. She should see this. Then she'd understand.' But when we were writing those names, I knew it would be a waste of time. She'll never change her mind. She's set in her thinking—and that kind of thinking is the reason we have things like the Holocaust in the first place."

"Do you want me to finish the names on your list?" I offer. "Maybe you should, uh, go relax or something."

He gives me a watery smile. "You're a good dude, Michael." And he heads back in to finish his links.

Pamela should see him transcribing names with such exquisite care, like he's cutting a diamond. None of the others leave, even though they were all finished twenty minutes ago. That's the impression the Florida survivors made on us.

It's a turning point for me, and I think everybody else too. We've been working on this chain for weeks, churning out millions of links on our journey to six million. But for the very first time, we don't see loops of construction paper.

We see faces.

CHAPTER TWENTY-SIX

LINCOLN ROWLEY

The first time Grandma visits since all this started is at Thanksgiving. This year it's our turn to host, so she and Grandpa drive in from Denver in one of the classic cars they collect. From my room upstairs, I can hear the 1962 engine roaring half a mile away. And when the old Cadillac pulls into our driveway, longer than a pontoon boat, with bigger fins than a great white shark, Mom and I run down to greet them.

Everything's the way it always is—the "shave and a haircut, two bits" blast of the horn and Grandpa's disbelief over how tall I am now. It's the usual reunion—until my eyes meet my grandmother's. I've seen Grandma a million times, but never before as a Holocaust survivor.

"Well, what do you know? We're in the presence of a celebrity," she says, indicating that she looks at me a little differently now too.

"We're reading a lot about you in the newspapers, Link," Grandpa adds proudly. "You get more coverage than the president, the pope, and the queen of England put together. All good stuff."

"Not all," Grandma counters with just a hint of the French accent that remains from her childhood in the orphanage. "Who is this ReelTok person? I can't get a sense of him. He seems to be anti-everything."

"He's a vlogger—a video blogger," I reply. "Our paper chain never could have gotten so famous without him."

She sighs. "I suppose that's always the goal these days. Everything has to be famous or it doesn't count. We all need our personal business splashed across the media. There's no such thing as privacy anymore."

Translation: Her story about being handed over to nuns to escape the Holocaust was her secret until her grandson exposed it to the world.

Come to think of it, nobody ever told me exactly how my grandparents reacted to this whole bar mitzvah thing. All Mom said was they were coming to the temple service. I just assumed that meant they were all in. Why wouldn't they be? They always came to my baseball games and basketball tournaments and soccer matches. They were there for the fifth-grade play and my elementary school graduation. I'm their only grandkid. This is the first time it occurs to me that a couple of lifelong churchgoers might feel pretty weird that their grandson is having a bar mitzvah.

I grab a suitcase in each arm, and we troop inside the house. Before we can make it to the guest room, Grandma freezes in the hall and I almost rear-end her. She's peering in the doorway to Dad's office, and I can already see what's caught her attention. Ever since news of my bar mitzvah has piggybacked on the paper chain story, Jewish communities from all around the country have been sending me stuff they think I'm going to need for the big day. Actually, I don't need any of it—Rabbi Gold says Temple Judea will supply everything for me. But it's pretty amazing how many people want to help me out. I now have sixteen prayer shawls, 158 kippot, two dozen leather-bound Hebrew prayer books, and nine ceremonial wine goblets, all piled on top of Dad's desk.

Grandma stares at the prayer shawl—Rabbi Gold told me it's called a tallit—draped over the back of the swivel chair. I recite the line of silver Hebrew writing embossed on the blue-and-white silk.

"What does that mean?" she asks.

"It's a prayer for when you put it on," I reply. "The rabbi calls it an ancient Jewish cheat sheet for people who can't remember the words."

"It's all Greek to me," puts in Grandpa with a snicker.

"Isn't it wonderful?" Mom asks pointedly. "Complete strangers are sending these things to Link via the school, just like they're sending thousands of paper chains."

"Amazing," Grandpa agrees.

"You've certainly got a lot of hats," Grandma comments. The stacked kippot completely cover Dad's scale model of the surrounding mountains, showing where Dino-land is supposed to go.

"They're called kippot, or yarmulkes," I tell her. "And that's nothing. This one guy is lending the temple a Torah that was rescued from the Nazis. He doesn't trust the mail, so he and his wife are driving it down personally from Toronto, Canada. He emailed last night from a Days Inn outside Indianapolis."

Grandma swallows hard. "You're . . . having some interesting experiences."

"First class!" Grandpa agrees heartily.

I normally love it when my grandparents visit, but today

it's pretty awkward. I was planning on giving them a bar mitzvah preview, since Dana says I'm getting good. But I don't think that's such a hot idea anymore. I can't really blame Grandma for being thrown by all this. I was pretty weirded out myself when Mom told me about the family history. And Mom was weirder still. So when you're the actual person it happened to, that has to be rough . . . even if you can't remember anything because you were a baby.

I'm sure it makes my family wonder: Grandma's my only connection to being Jewish, so if she's against it, why am I doing it? Sure, I'm honoring my relatives who died in the Holocaust and the cousins who were never born. But just like Grandma, I never knew those people. I live in the here and now, with friends who say I'm no fun anymore. And a father who's going along with my plans not because he wants to, but in spite of the fact that he'd rather be doing almost anything else. Worse, he's convinced that his dream of Dino-land is being ruined by all the focus on the Holocaust, the swastikas, and Chokecherry's past. And Mom? She's my biggest booster, but in the end, who knows how she really feels deep down?

Dad comes home from work early and drops his briefcase beside the desk in his office. "I see the yarmulke express made another delivery," he comments before greeting Grandma and Grandpa.

Everybody laughs a little too much at his joke.

Except Grandma. "I guess you've gotten used to all this, George."

"Oh, you never get used to it." Then he adds, "Have you heard Link practice? In the space of a couple of months, he's picked up what it takes most kids years to learn. It's a good sign for his future."

My father listens to me practice? Since when?

For dinner we go to Angelino's, where Grandpa loves the baked ziti. The traffic is slow on Main Street, not because Chokecherry is big enough to have a rush hour, but because the cars have to snake around the parked trucks and plows.

"This is ridiculous," Grandpa complains. "It used to take three minutes to get from one side of town to the other."

The reason the service vehicles are out on the road looms up on the right—the municipal garage. Even from a distance you can see through the glass doors that the entire building is packed to the rafters with multicolored paper chain.

Grandma draws in a sharp breath. "Is that—?"

"That's only a little bit," I supply. "The whole thing would be hundreds of miles long. It's all over town, in warehouses, silos, basements, and attics."

Grandpa pulls up behind a road grader, and the five of us get out and approach the garage. There are other people there too, just standing and looking. We end up next to a family from Shadbush Crossing who drove a hundred miles to see it.

They've got a little kid with them—a boy, maybe four or five years old, his eyes wide with wonder. His whole body is pressed against the window as if he's trying to make himself a part of the landscape of colored paper loops inside.

"How many do you think are in there?" he asks breathlessly.

"At least half a million," I tell him. "But that's barely a tenth of what we've got. We're almost up to five million links now."

He pulls away to beam at me, and the next thing I know, my quiet, reserved grandmother steps right up to the glass to drink in the paper chain and everything it represents. It might be a trick of the light, but I'm pretty sure I spot a small tear running down her cheek.

I take her hand. "Want to get a closer look?" I whisper.

She regards me questioningly, but follows along. I lead her around the side of the building to the employees' back entrance. I push the door open, and we pass through a locker room and step out into the main garage—at least as far as we can, because the place is jammed with floor-to-ceiling paper chain. We might as well be underwater. The multicolored loops are right up against our faces and fill in over our heads as we move.

Grandma's breath quickens, and I wonder if I've made a mistake bringing her in here. She's an old lady, and I'm practically drowning her in chain. I make a move to lead her back outside, but she stops me.

She says, "At the convent, we all wondered about our parents and why they'd left us with the Sisters of Sainte Hilaire. The nuns were kind, but they were absolutely tight-lipped about our families. German soldiers searched regularly. Young girls couldn't be trusted to keep secrets, so the sisters made sure we had none. And when the war was over, nobody looked for parents. It was all we could do to look for food."

I'm deadly silent. My grandmother has never opened up to me like this before. For all I know, she's never even said these things to Mom. Grandma may have escaped the horrors of the Holocaust, but she didn't get off scot-free.

She goes on. "I was seventy-three years old when I finally learned the truth about my parents, my family. I can only imagine their anguish when their one hope for any kind of future was to save the life of their infant daughter. But how could I grieve for them? They didn't have faces. No names, no voices to remember. Sure, I understood that the way I was raised was not the way my natural parents would have raised me. It was life-changing—yet I was too old to change. I was born Jewish . . . but it's not who I am. At my age, it's too late for me to be anyone else."

She takes a tremulous breath. "I wasn't able to mourn my parents, because I couldn't see them." She holds up her arms. "Now I know that they're here, among the links of your wonderful chain. And what you're doing, this bar mitzvah, is to reclaim my family. *Our* family. You've done something for me that I never could have done for myself. And I love you so much for it."

She hugs me, and the sudden movement triggers a mini avalanche in the paper loops that fill the building. Chain half buries us, but we barely notice. At that moment, I feel closer to my grandmother than I ever have.

It's a really emotional moment . . . until the "shave and a haircut, two bits" horn of Grandpa's car blares from outside.

"I guess that means we're taking too long," I snicker.

"And he's hungry," she confirms.

By the time we wrestle our way out of the garage, we're both smiling.

CHAPTER TWENTY-SEVEN

CAROLINE MCNUTT

You can taste the coming winter in the air. It gets colder every week. And winter is really winter where we live.

The kids at Chokecherry Middle School don't care. We don't even notice. School spirit keeps you warm no matter what the temperature is.

If I don't get elected eighth-grade president next year in a landslide, it'll be a crime against student government. As much as Daniel Faraz may try to take credit for the paper chain, everybody knows the seventh grade took the lead on this one. And who's in charge of the seventh grade? Caroline McNutt, that's who. You're welcome, world.

And it is the whole world now. We've been interviewed by media outlets from four different continents (what's the problem, Australia?). ReelTok is up nearly a million followers ever since he moved to Chokecherry to report on our story. We've received donations of supplies and paper chains from all fifty states plus eleven other countries. You think a little cold weather and a few flurries can stop us now? Godzilla couldn't stop us now!

Shivering in my jacket, I'm supervising a group of kids unloading a cube van with Illinois plates. Most of our donations come packed in cartons. But when we open the van, we find the back jammed with chain. Sophie grabs one end, and we start pulling it out. She's halfway to the parking lot before I realize that the entire payload is a single endless line of connected paper links. Pretty soon, all my volunteers are stretched back and forth across the front of the school, while the unbroken chain rustles in the cold wind.

Suddenly, Michael explodes out the front door, waving his clipboard and shouting, "What are you doing? I still have to count those!"

"There weren't any boxes," I explain. "When we opened up the van, all this was in the back."

The driver hands me an envelope with the logo of an elementary school in Buffalo Grove, Illinois. I open it, and Michael and I read the letter inside.

> Dear Chokecherry Middle School,
>   We can't tell you what an inspiration your message of tolerance and remembrance has been to us. Our students have been coming in early every morning for the past three weeks to work on our paper chain to add to yours. Please attach these 1,986 links to your . . .

Michael draws in a wheeze of ice-cold air that must be painful.

"Are you okay?" I ask him.

He pulls out his phone and keys numbers rapidly into the

calculator function. Then he wheels and pounds up the steps and back into the school.

"Wait here!" I tell my crew. "And don't pull too hard on the chain. You don't want to rip it!" I take off after Michael.

I catch up with him at the library, which is packed with paper-chainers, busily cutting and gluing.

"Stop!" he barks. "Stop working!"

"Michael, what's going on?" I demand.

Wordlessly, he shoves his phone under my nose. The number on the calculator reads: 6,000,023.

"We did it," he croaks. "Six million. We hit six million!"

The roar that rises from the assembled paper-chainers very nearly raises the roof. For an instant, glue sticks, scissors, and construction paper are airborne, hanging like a cloud over the library. Then it's all raining down on us as we embrace one another and dance like maniacs. A bottle of Elmer's glue bounces off my head as I'm hugging Michael, and it actually hurts. But who cares? All I can think of is that this makes me the greatest seventh-grade president in the history of student government. Those hard times when Chokecherry Middle School couldn't sell enough raffle tickets to even pay for the prize might as well be a hundred years ago. This is the top. The pinnacle.

One minute we're all going nuts with pure joy at hitting six million, and then we all get quiet as we remember what that number represents. We're still cheering inside, but we're also thinking about six million lives snuffed out by the worst kind of evil the world has ever known. It's not the same rah-rah celebration, but just the idea of the statement we've made fills us with pride. Dana stands with her hands clasped and her head bowed respectfully, and the rest of us take our lead from her.

Mr. Brademas rushes into the library. "What's all the noise about? What's going on?" He looks around, bewildered because there isn't any noise. We're motionless and solemn.

In answer, Michael shows him the number on his phone calculator.

Our staid, dignified principal blurts, "No way!"

"Yes way!" Pouncey bellows right in his face.

And the party starts up again, led by Mr. Brademas.

I remember that I left a group of kids outside in the cold with the paper chain that put us over the top. By the time I run down to get them, the text messages are flying all around the school and throughout town. As I pass the gym, a volleyball game is interrupted, and the players from both teams give me a round of applause. Kids high-five me in the hall. Even the detention room echoes with shouts of triumph, which grow even louder when Mrs. Lemay lets everyone go early. I get swarmed and thanked by kids who are usually bombarding me with spitballs.

When at last I make it outside, our final strand of chain is frosted with snow, so I make everybody go downstairs and stand near the furnace to thaw it out.

Michael and Dana find me there, sweating in my coat and sniffling a little from the emotion of what we've accomplished. It would be emotional for anyone in student government. But it counts double for me, since I've never had an accomplishment before—despite my many years of trying. It's a really big deal.

"We're going to see ReelTok," Michael informs me. "Someone should let him know we hit six million."

"Mostly, we're going to tell him to leave," Dana adds pointedly. "If the paper chain project is over, so is his excuse for camping out across the street from our school."

Camping out isn't a bad way to describe the vlogger these days. Now that the first bite of winter is here, he's pitched a tent around his usual spot in the park, and he has a space heater that runs off a small portable generator that sits on the other side of the canvas. You can hear the put-putting halfway across town. It's so loud that he has to shut it down when he does interviews and records his videos—not that there are as many interviews now that the weather has changed.

Michael tries to knock on one of the tent poles, but there's no chance he can be heard over the generator. So I poke my head inside the tent flap. "Mr. Tok?"

The vlogger huddles in his parka in front of the space heater. By a strange coincidence—or maybe not—he looks eerily like he does on YouTube, since his voluminous scarf and ski hat cover his face everywhere except the letterbox view from eyes to lower lip.

I always feel weird when I see him, because of the terrible things he's said about our town. On the other hand, it's thanks to his vlog and website that news of our paper chain spread so far and wide. So without him, there's no way my student government career ever could have reached the summit I hit today.

Spying us, ReelTok reaches outside the tent and switches off the generator. "What's up, kidlets?"

"We've got news!" I announce, relishing the big reveal.

"Yeah, yeah," he yawns. "You made your six million. Congratulations."

Michael stares at him. "How could you know so fast?"

He waves his phone at us. "TokNation has eyes everywhere."

I don't know why I'm surprised. He's always going on about TokNation like it's his personal CIA. But come to think of it, this probably just came from one of our classmates posting it on ReelTok.com. Most of the kids were already fans even before the guy moved into the park across the street. The urge to be first to tell Adam Tok would have been irresistible.

Dana speaks up. "So you know. I guess that means you'll be leaving town soon."

The vlogger beams at her. "Trying to get rid of me so fast? I thought you were grateful for all the publicity I've brought you."

"We are! We are!" I break in. "We never could have gotten to six million without the attention you brought us."

"It's just that, you know," Dana goes on, "now that the paper chain is over, I just figured—"

"You assume that the paper chain is what brought me here." ReelTok clucks. "I expected more from the daughter of two PhDs."

"How do you know who my parents are?" Dana asks sharply.

"When you have seventeen million followers, they tell you an awful lot about an awful lot. You're Dana Levinson, your parents are here with Wexford-Smythe University, and you're the only Jewish kid at Chokecherry Middle School."

"Not true!" Dana snaps.

"Right. Lincoln Rowley. Well played."

"If it wasn't for the paper chain, why *did* you come here?" Michael asks the vlogger.

"I'm glad you asked," ReelTok replies pleasantly. "The paper chain was my *excuse* for coming here. But the *story* was always Chokecherry itself. I live in a big city, and that's an easy target for haters. *Oh, the traffic! Oh, the crime! The rude people! The pollution! The garbage!* But I always knew that if you scratch any small town, you find the same and even worse. So when I heard about swastikas in a middle school and a KKK past that nobody will even talk about, much less admit to, I knew Chokecherry was the story I'd been dreaming about."

I don't know what to say. I always looked the other way when ReelTok put down our town, because his vlog was so important to the paper chain. I was thinking like the seventh-grade president, and our project needed him. But now I have to wonder what we did to make him hate us so much. I look over at Michael, and he seems pretty confused too.

"Fine," Dana tells him. "You got your story. We're all awful. So why don't you just buzz off?"

"Because my story's not over yet. I'm just about to post a new interview. Interested in a little preview?"

"No," Dana says flatly. "Everybody around here has already seen more from your YouTube channel than they need." She turns to Michael and me. "Come on, guys. We're out of here."

Smiling even wider, ReelTok opens his laptop. "Oh, you're going to want to stick around for this one. It's definitely worth your time."

CHAPTER TWENTY-EIGHT

REELTOK

From the YouTube channel of Adam Tok

Interview with Lincoln Rowley

REELTOK: Your bar mitzvah's only a week away.
Getting excited? Nervous, maybe?
LINK: A little bit of both. I Zoomed with Rabbi Gold
last night. He says I'm ready.
REELTOK: That's good. And now that the swastikas
are a thing of the past, you must be even more
relaxed.
LINK: Relaxed?
REELTOK: You know, a Jewish ceremony with anti-
Semitic symbols popping up all over the place. It's
a good thing Pamela Bynes was caught before she
could do any more damage.
LINK: I feel bad for her. She's my friend.
REELTOK: See, I find that confusing. How could
a kid who's just discovered his Jewish heritage be
friends with someone who did what she did? Is it
because you believe her story about not doing the

first swastika? Do you feel that she's a little less guilty because she didn't start all this?

LINK: I don't know.

REELTOK: Really? A Jewish boy like you doesn't know how you feel about something like that?

LINK: I haven't known about the Jewish thing for very . . . I mean, it's a lot of change really fast.

REELTOK: I want to tell you a little story. When the weather was first starting to cool off, I got arrested for lighting a fire in the park—the local cops aren't my biggest fans. You know how they caught me? That house across the square—number sixty-two. They have one of those video security doorbells. They saw my fire on the live camera feed and ratted me out to the police.

LINK: So you got the tent and the heater.

REELTOK: You're missing the point. The minute I found out about that camera, I realized it looks clear across the park . . . all the way to the school. You know?

LINK: I guess.

REELTOK: Don't you see? That doorbell camera is like video surveillance on the school. I wasn't here when the first swastika was painted . . . but the doorbell was. So it might be interesting to look at the video feed from that day. You know, to see if Pamela is lying about that.

LINK: But wait—those people just let you come into their house and watch their footage?

REELTOK: Not necessary. When you've got seventeen million followers, it's never hard to find a competent hacker who's willing to do you a favor. Anyway, the news is, Pamela is telling the truth. She left practice with the other cheerleaders around five.

LINK: Okay . . .

REELTOK: I also saw Michael Amorosa bike up and enter the school a little before seven thirty. That's consistent with when the first swastika was reported found. Between five o'clock and then, only one person entered that building. Would you like to tell me who it was?

LINK: How could I possibly know that?

REELTOK: Because it was you.

CHAPTER TWENTY-NINE

LINCOLN ROWLEY

The crazy part is, I never thought twice about what I spray-painted at the school. My mind was a couple of hours ahead on the dinosaur poop gag we were about to play on the scientists' office at the strip mall. That was the one with all the moving parts: Jordie, Pouncey, the girls, not to mention an eighty-pound bag of smelly fertilizer that wasn't exactly easy to cart around town.

So why did I do it? Why do I do anything? If I knew that, maybe I could stop. I'm not a thinker; I'm a doer. I went from learning about Grandma to bar mitzvah lessons in the blink of an eye. I'm having a bar mitzvah on Saturday . . . or maybe I'm not. Now that the word is out that I painted the first swastika, I can't picture myself being super welcome inside any synagogue.

I was ticked off. No question about that. Dad had just yanked me off the soccer team and the lectures were fast and furious, not to mention loud and long. It was George Rowley's greatest hits, played on an endless loop. I was hearing about my future eighteen times a day. I needed an outlet before my head exploded. I wanted revenge. We had the fertilizer thing planned, but that was too funny. I wanted something unfunny, something that would freak people out.

When I snuck into the school that day, I honestly had no idea what I was going to paint on the atrium wall. Just the fact that I was painting it—that was my statement. This wouldn't be any goofy gag like I usually do; nothing that could be laughed off or ignored as "kids being kids." It would be vandalism, plain and ugly, defacement of school property. I could just as easily have painted *I'M ANGRY*.

Oh, how I wish I had.

Even when I pressed down on the button to start the spray, I still didn't know. The swastika practically painted itself. It said *angry* just as if the word was right up there. Dad was worried about my future? I was giving him something to worry about. More than one thing, in fact. I was saying: *Here's your perfect town, George Rowley! Here's the next Orlando—a place so awesome it's a shoo-in for Dino-land!*

I knew a swastika was a nasty thing, but I swear I didn't realize *how* nasty. To me, it was anti-everything . . . which was how I felt at that moment. If you'd asked me about Nazi Germany, I would have remembered swastikas on tanks and airplanes from World War II movies. And, yeah, we did that Holocaust unit in fifth grade. But that was facts, numbers, a quiz at the end. It didn't really sink in.

I wanted to *shock*. It honestly never occurred to me that it would hurt people. Or scare them. Which is no excuse. None of this is an excuse. I'm only trying to explain—to myself, more than anyone else.

What was I thinking?

I *wasn't* thinking. It's the most thoughtless, heedless, brainless thing I've ever done.

Which is how anger works. And also how hate works. I didn't hate—and I don't. But on that day, those two just crashed together in me.

No excuses.

So here I am, the most despised person in Chokecherry. I can't say I blame anybody. I'm not even surprised by what's happened to me. I already saw it happen to Pamela. I'm suspended indefinitely from school. I've been arrested on a vandalism charge. Our lawyer says I probably won't have to go to juvie, but for sure I'm going to end up with some kind of community service. I don't see how that's going to work. No one in *this* community is ever going to let me get close enough to do any kind of service. And thanks to ReelTok's giant community of followers, I'm reviled all around the world. I might be able to get a gig in Antarctica, keeping the eggs warm for the penguin dads, but that's about it.

That sounds smart-alecky, but trust me, there's nothing funny about being me right now. I've always been pretty popular—I guess because I've got attitude and I'm good at sports and pulling pranks. I didn't care about that—at least I thought I didn't. But now that it's gone, man, do I miss it. I don't need to be loved. But being hated—I mean *really* hated—is truly awful.

I can't even blame them for hating me. I pretty much hate myself. Don't forget: They just found out about me. I've known from Day One. You think it was easy sitting through all that tolerance education, learning every day that the bad thing I did was a thousand times worse than I thought it was? And when the other swastikas started appearing—even though I wasn't doing them, I understood that they were my fault, because I started it. Every NO PLACE FOR HATE sign was aimed directly at me. If our school had become a place for hate, that was 100 percent my doing. And when I learned Grandma's story, I couldn't even look at myself in the mirror.

I wasn't lying when I said my bar mitzvah was a tribute to my family killed during the Holocaust and the scores of relatives who never got the chance to be born. I felt that. I *still* feel that, more than ever. That was only half the story, though. As soon as Dana spoke those two words—*bar mitzvah*—I saw a lifeline, a way to make up for what I'd done, even just a little. I get that she was kidding. Why should she see me as Jewish? I'm not certain I see myself that way—it's hard to shift gears after being something else your whole life. But I knew I had to try.

It was hard at first. All those Hebrew words and sounds seemed so alien, and I had so much history and tradition to catch up on. But Rabbi Gold was super supportive, and once Dana started working with me, I really turned the corner. I'm *proud* of how far I've come. But now, the whole bar mitzvah thing is only making people hate me more. The kid who suddenly presents himself as Jewish secretly did the most anti-Jewish thing ever. What's up with that? Like it's just another one of my pranks—and this one's on the whole town.

Even the paper chain, great as it is, only makes me look worse. Not that it was my thing, or even my idea. But somehow my bar mitzvah and the project got rolled up together in people's minds. Maybe it was *Link* and *links*, you know? Whatever the reason, our whole town is buried under 378 miles of paper chain, and it all started with a swastika—painted by the ultimate flimflam artist, me.

Out of six hundred kids who can't stand me, the one I regret the most is Dana. I guess I deserve her hating me more than anybody. She didn't take me 100 percent seriously, but she helped me anyway. She was nice to me and so were her parents, even though they knew I did the dinosaur poop thing. Now that I'm kicked out of school, I don't even have the chance to talk to her, to try to explain the unexplainable. I did see her once downtown, when my folks were taking me to visit our lawyer. The look she gave me would have fricasseed a rhino. I tried to call her and got a message that her phone was "not accepting calls." I think that means I've been blocked.

I keep hoping, though. One night I have to run to ransack the couch cushions for my ringing phone and pick up without checking first to see who it is.

"Dana?" I ask breathlessly.

"Link?" It's only one syllable, but I recognize the girl's voice immediately. It isn't Dana. It's just about the polar opposite of Dana. Suddenly, I'm very much aware of the hair on the back of my neck, and it's standing at full attention.

"Pamela," I breathe.

"I had to talk to you," she tells me urgently.

"Why?" At this moment, I can't imagine another human wanting anything to do with me. Not even her.

She seems surprised by the question. "Because you're the only one who *understands*."

That's when it hits me—Pamela and I have something in common. We both painted swastikas. She thinks we're on the same team.

"I did something stupid," I tell her. "You did something hateful. And you kept on doing it even after you saw how it was affecting people."

"Which was the whole point," she insists. "It's like everybody's asleep in this town. It took *you* to wake us up. To wake *me* up."

I always understood that my swastika inspired the others, but to hear it straight from Pamela's mouth is devastating. The way she explains it, I'm practically the pied piper of racist symbols.

I thought nothing could make me feel lower than I already do. I stand corrected.

"How can you say all this, Pamela?" I demand, an uncomfortable quaver in my voice. "You know about my family. My grandmother . . ."

"That makes you the perfect messenger," she reasons. "Nobody would ever suspect you."

A dozen arguments pop into my head. Like the fact that I didn't know about Grandma when I painted that first swastika. Or the obvious truth that her "perfect messenger" got caught just the same as she did.

But I don't say those things, because I have nothing to say to Pamela. My actions were inexcusable; hers were worse. And the most terrible part of all is that she honestly has no clue that she did anything wrong. Maybe it's not her fault, coming from a family with connections to the KKK. That's how racism survives from generation to generation. I can't control that. What I *can* control is that she's not going to be my problem anymore.

"I'm hanging up now, Pamela," I tell her. "I'm sorry for the way things turned out."

She starts yelling, but by that time, my phone is off my ear. All that comes through is a stream of rapid-fire chirping.

I end the call, secure in the knowledge that I'll never speak to Pamela Bynes again.

The only friends I'm still in contact with are Jordie and Pouncey. By the time they show up on Wednesday, my parents are so glad to see I'm not a total outcast that they send them right up to my room. It's not that Mom and Dad forgive me—they don't. They don't even forgive *themselves* for what a jerk I've turned out to be. But the shouting stage is finally over and we've moved on to figuring out how we're going to survive this. That's right in Dad's wheelhouse: my future, which doesn't look so bright anymore. It's also not lost on him that being father to the notorious swastika vandal isn't a good look for the guy who's trying to find investors for Dino-land and turn Chokecherry into the next Orlando.

To be honest, I get a little choked up while Jordie, Pouncey, and I are bro-hugging and punching at each other's shoulders. It proves that the world didn't end for me, at least not completely.

"Thanks for coming, you guys," I tell them. "I honestly didn't think I had a friend left in the world."

"Yeah, well, if anybody asks, I was never here," Jordie says seriously. "My folks banned me from you."

"Mine didn't," Pouncey puts in. "Mostly because they don't care what I do. Seriously, I told them I was going to see Jack the Ripper. My mom said, 'Have a good time.'"

"I think Jack the Ripper is more popular than I am around here these days." I sigh. "The worst part is I totally understand why."

Pouncey nods wisely. "You really stepped in it this time. You're making me look good, and that's not easy. I'm usually the one Jordie's not allowed to talk to."

"What's everybody saying at school?" I ask. "I guess I'm not getting elected homecoming king anytime soon, right?"

"People are pretty mad," Jordie agrees. "Mostly, though, they just don't get it. One minute, you're Kid Bar Mitzvah, and the next you're Swastika Guy? You can't blame them for being confused. *I'm* confused."

"I'm confused too," I admit. "But take my word for it: If I could go back in time and undo it, I would. Honestly, I didn't know it's possible to feel so bad in so many ways all at the same time. I feel bad for doing it. I feel bad for keeping you guys in the dark. I even feel kind of weird about Pamela. She probably never would have started if it hadn't been for me."

Jordie studies his sneakers.

"Yeah, yeah, and you steered the *Titanic* into that iceberg too," Pouncey scolds me. "The whole world's dumping on you. Why would you dump on yourself?"

I shake my head. "Guys, I know we used to joke about getting kicked out of school, but when it really happens, it's no fun. If I get expelled, I'll have to go to boarding school somewhere. Or we'll have to move. Seriously, I'd give anything to have Brademas yell at me one more time."

"Dude, take your temperature," Pouncey cautions. "I hope you're not contagious."

"What are you going to do?" Jordie asks me. "You're supposed to be having a bar mitzvah on Saturday. That can't still happen, right?"

That's the biggest question of all. For months, my life has been about one thing—the bar mitzvah. And here I am, 100 percent ready and knocking on the door—and I have no idea if it's going to happen, or if it even should.

Issue 1: Am I welcome at Temple Judea? I don't have any synagogue experience beyond Zooming Rabbi Gold, but how can their congregation not hate me after what I did? I can't even hope they haven't heard. Everybody heard. ReelTok made sure of that.

Issue 2: Why would my parents let me go through with it? It was hard enough for them to sign on to this plan in the first place. A swastika really doesn't fit in with the rest of it. Is this supposed to be another one of the pranks I'm infamous for? If so, this one's not just on them, but on a whole school, a whole town, and a whole religion.

Issue 3: Even if I do go ahead with the bar mitzvah, who'd come? My official friend count is down to two—and one of them has to keep it a secret that he associates with me. Besides my parents, who'd be there? No one from Chokecherry. Maybe my grandparents. I called Grandma to apologize when the ReelTok interview came out, and she says she forgives me. I hope that's true. I couldn't tell from her voice over the phone. I feel horrible for taking something really strange and emotional from her life and making it even weirder.

What a mess—and I genuinely have nobody to blame but myself.

Dad ends the call and sets his phone down on his desk, leaning it against one of the yarmulke towers. "That was the synagogue office. They say to get to the temple by nine on Saturday morning."

"No way!" I exclaim. "That's all? Nothing about—you know—*it*? Everything that's happened?"

"Maybe they haven't heard," Mom muses. "Not everybody follows your ReelTok, especially a religious community."

I shrug. "Maybe, but I doubt it. Thanks to the paper chain hitting six million, Chokecherry is all over the news these days—and so is this story." I look from Dad to Mom and back to Dad again. "I'm so sorry, you guys. You supported me all the way, and I ruined everything. This screwup might even hurt Dino-land!"

My father says the last thing I expect: "Who cares about Dino-land?"

I stare at him. "*You* care about Dino-land! It's the most important thing in your career! You invested all that time! All that money!"

"The most important thing in my career isn't as important as my son," Dad declares.

Mom puts a hand on my shoulder. "We're your parents, Link. We love you. The instant you were born, we were on your side, no matter what."

In a way, that only makes me feel worse for letting them down. But it also feels kind of good to feel that bad for the right reasons.

"It's not going to be easy, but we'll get through this as a family," Mom goes on. "Right now, though, there's a decision to be made about Saturday. And you're the only one who can make it."

I think it over. There's no way Rabbi Gold doesn't know about the swastika. He's probably testing me to see if I'll confess. That's the first thing they tell you about having a bar mitzvah—you're supposed to be becoming a man.

That's what I have to do—man up.

I take a deep breath. "I'm calling Rabbi Gold."

Rabbi Gold has a deep, resonant voice so that even when he says hello, it sounds like he's making a major pronouncement from the pulpit. It intimidated me at first, until I realized what a nice guy he is.

"It's Lincoln Rowley," I identify myself. "You know, from this Saturday."

He seems amused. "Even at my age, I usually remember kids I've been working with for months. What can I do for you?"

I swallow hard. "I have to tell you something. And when you hear it, you're not going to want to let me in your synagogue anymore."

He says, "You're about to confess that you painted a swastika in the hallway of your school." In the awkward silence he adds, "I'm in Shadbush Crossing, not Mars. Yes, of course I've heard. Would you like to tell me why you would do such a thing?"

It's out in the open now. I'm talking about the worst thing I ever did to the person best qualified to know how awful it is.

"I don't have an excuse," I admit. "I didn't paint that symbol because my hand slipped. I did it on purpose. The only thing I can say in my own defense is that I honestly wasn't trying to be anti-Semitic or racist. I was trying to be a jerk. I don't know if that's much better, but it's the truth."

"And this intention to be a jerk," the rabbi prompts, "did you succeed?"

"Man, did I ever!" I practically groan. "But the worst part is, I inspired a real racist to paint even more swastikas. Then things got out of control. The swastikas brought out stories about Chokecherry's past, and suddenly, neighbors were fighting over whether all that had really happened—just like trolls on the internet say the Holocaust is made up. A swastika may be just a symbol, but it's amazing how much trouble it can cause once it gets inside people's heads."

I tell him the whole story—everything that happened, and as much of the why as I can figure out. When I'm finished, Rabbi Gold is silent for a long time, and I hang on, actually shaking. I never realized how much I want him to like me— especially now that almost nobody else does.

At long last, he says, "Thank you for having the courage to come to me like this. That speaks to your character as much as anything else you might have done. And while all this began with a horrible error in judgment, it gave rise to something remarkable—a paper chain of six million links, representing six million lives tragically lost to us in the Holocaust."

"That wasn't all me," I confess. "I mean, I helped, but it was our whole school, our whole town, the whole country and beyond. Almost everybody pitched in once they found out about it. Art supply companies sent us materials. Delivery services brought us paper chains from all around the world. It's unbelievable how big it got."

"It's not unbelievable," the rabbi informs me, his voice softening. "It's the way human beings *ought* to be. Link, there hasn't been time for me to give you much of a formal Jewish education. But you might remember from Sunday school some of the stories of the Old Testament. God forgives us—and by doing that, God shows us how to forgive each other. Even more important, those of us who've been forgiven spend the rest of our lives trying to be worthy of that forgiveness."

Rabbi Gold has a way of looking at things that's different from anybody else I've ever met. For the first time since ReelTok outed me, I begin to toy with the possibility that I'm not the worst person in the history of the planet.

"And in that spirit," he goes on, "be at the temple by nine a.m. Saturday and we'll do this right."

So there it is. Rabbi Gold isn't going to stand in my way. My parents are supporting me. I was so positive that the whole thing was going to be off that I never asked myself what *I* thought the right thing to do would be.

Now it's all up to me. I've got permission from everybody that matters—except myself. And I have to make up my mind before this call ends.

Do I deserve a bar mitzvah on Saturday?

Absolutely not.

But do I want to go through with it?

"Lincoln?" the rabbi prompts. "Are you still there?"

Even after everything that's happened, with me being a complete idiot, and knowing that no one's going to be there to support me, I want to do this.

"Yes, Rabbi. Thank you. I'll be there."

My parents are still in the office. Dad's on his computer, and Mom is nervously rearranging our yarmulke collection. Both look up as I step into the room.

I shoot them a shaky thumbs-up. "We're on."

CHAPTER THIRTY

DANA LEVINSON

The first time I set foot in Chokecherry, Colorado, I thought I'd been banished to Devil's Island. It was too small, too isolated, too far away from all my friends. The local kids were unwelcoming beyond belief. They made the scientists' families feel like unwanted intruders. I told my parents that it didn't matter to me if they found a live Stegosaurus knocking down telephone poles with its spiky tail, much less the droppings of a long-dead one. I wanted out. I was just that unhappy.

I didn't know the half of it.

If I never hear the name Link Rowley again, it's still going to be too soon. No, scratch that. I *won't* hear that name again. Even if somebody ties me to a chair, sticks headphones on me, and pipes *"Link Rowley! Link Rowley!"* in an endless loop at top volume, I will train my brain to block it out.

I have never felt so betrayed. So dirty. So *used*. When I think of the hours I spent training that creep to get ready for his "bar mitzvah," I could beat myself over the head with something. While I worked hard so he wouldn't make a fool of himself, he must have been laughing at me inside. It wasn't enough for him to deface our school with a swastika. He had to string along the stupid Jewish girl with that phony story about his grandmother

203

and the Holocaust. Worst of all, he pretended to be as outraged as the rest of us while Pamela went on her own swastika streak, when the whole time, *he* was the one who'd started it.

And now we have a paper chain 378 miles long—an astounding achievement for any town. The *Guinness Book of World Records* keeps calling Mayor Radisson to set up a time to come to Chokecherry to witness it officially for their book. But instead of being rightfully proud, everybody just feels like suckers, thanks to Link.

There was a time that I even stopped hating Chokecherry because we were involved in something unique and wonderful and we "egglets" were right in the thick of it. When Link was coming over practically every day so I could help him study—and even getting to know my family—I thought I'd found a real friend. Forget that. If something seems too good to be true, it usually is. Link's first contact with my family was to dump fertilizer on us. Well, it continued just like that . . . and the stink keeps getting worse and worse.

I can't stand being at school, even though there's no chance of running into Link, because he's been booted out. The only good part is that ReelTok has folded up his tent and is no longer staking out the school from the park across the street. Supposedly, he hasn't left town yet. He's been seen at his hotel and at a few local restaurants, and his rental car has been spotted around the area. He's still vlogging from Chokecherry, but I wouldn't watch that if you paid me. On the jerk scale, he's not much lower than Link.

It's funny—the school is no different from what it was at

the beginning of the year. There are no swastikas because Link and Pamela are both gone. And there's no paper chain either, since that's been farmed out all over town. But the effect of the last couple of months hangs over the building like a bad smell. It's not that people are ashamed of it. But no one wants to think about it because it brings up Link and Pamela and the swastikas and stories of what happened forty years ago. Instead of an accomplishment, it's turned into an embarrassment. And when the subject does come up, you hear a lot of grumbling about what a waste of time and energy and paper, and before you know it, a couple of kids are arguing over whether or not the Night of a Thousand Flames really happened.

It's breaking Michael's heart. For all his complaining, he nurtured that chain from the very first links all the way to six million. As for Caroline, I think she's on the verge of a break-down. After so many weeks of cutting and looping, gluing and volunteering, you couldn't get the kids here to show up for a school activity if you were handing out gold bars. Now that she sees all that progress evaporating, the seventh-grade president is afraid she'll never have a chance to be eighth-grade president. She's even talking about extending the paper chain another five million links in memory of the victims of the Holocaust who *weren't* Jewish. No takers. Chokecherry Middle School is paper-chained out. I've started hating every minute I'm at that place.

One morning, I wake up just as Dad is leaving for the elementary school with Ryan.

"What happened to my alarm?" I holler downstairs.

"I turned it off," Mom calls up to me. "Your father and I are worried about you, Dana. We've decided you could use a mental health day off school."

I don't love them minding my business, but I've got to admit that sounds like a pretty great idea.

"I'm all right," I tell Mom once I've managed to drag myself to the kitchen. "I just wish Dad could dig up the rest of those dinosaurs so we could move out of this town. Even the North Pole would be an improvement. Walruses don't carve swastikas into the ice with their tusks. At least I think they don't."

My mother sighs. "You know your father and me well enough to understand that nothing ever happens fast in the world of paleontology."

I groan. "The fossils are a hundred million years old. Why does it take longer than that to dig them out of the ground?"

"It only seems longer," Mom says patiently. "Speaking of fossils, that's what Dad and I have in mind for you today. When's the last time you went on a dig?"

My vision of this glorious day off darkens a little. It's not that I don't like the digs. What could be cooler than unearthing an ancient bone that's been hidden for tens of millions of years? But anything that old is so fragile, so delicate that getting it out of the ground without smashing it is a weeks-long process of picking and stroking at it with a shrimp fork and a paintbrush. Not exactly high-action stuff.

Dad comes back from delivering Ryan, and we head out. First, we drop Mom off at the office in town. I swear I can still smell the fertilizer in that place even though that incident was two months ago. Which reminds me that Link should have been the prime swastika suspect right from the start. Nobody else gets such joy from doing stupid, destructive things. I guess I can't blame Chokecherry for that—this isn't the only town to give some juvenile delinquent a free pass because he happens to be popular and good at sports. Anyway, Link seems to have run out of free passes with this latest stunt. Nobody forgives swastikas.

It's about a twenty-minute ride into the mountains to what Wexford-Smythe University calls the Shadbush County Excavation Site.

Dad rolls down the windows. "Smell that air."

I pull my coat tighter around me. "It's too cold."

"Lighten up, Dana. You don't forfeit your right to complain if you admit there are a few nice things about Colorado."

I smile in spite of myself. Nothing smells as clean as cold mountain air, and the views are really beautiful.

We veer off onto a dirt road that ends at a small parking area. There are a few other cars and a food truck with cooking smells coming from the metal chimney. A five-minute walk through the trees leads us to a huge clearing about the size of two football fields. There are half a dozen spots where scientists, in hard hats, gloves, and safety glasses are down in the rock and dirt, working. It's as quiet as a chess tournament except for the clinking of hammers, the shaking of sieves, and the low buzz of conversation between colleagues. There are cartons of varying sizes and a large roll of foam wrap.

"I kind of expected to see a giant Triceratops skeleton carved halfway out of the ground," I comment.

My father laughs. "No such luck. If we come up with a fragment of bone the size of a golf ball, it's a big deal. And it wouldn't be from a Triceratops anyway. That's a Cretaceous animal. All our findings so far have been from the Jurassic period."

"Even the poop?" I ask with a smirk.

"Believe it or not, droppings don't come stamped with a species label," Dad deadpans. "But the samples we've had dated are consistent with the bones we've found."

Watching paleontologists pulling things out of the ground—mostly worms—isn't A-list entertainment. After the first couple of hours of nothing, you stop waiting for somebody to yell "Eureka!" and haul a Brachiosaurus femur out of the dirt, holding it over their head like the Stanley Cup. When I complain that I'm bored, Dad gives me a paintbrush and sits me down so I can "help." I'm pretty far from everybody else, though, so it's obvious that's he's put me where I can't do any harm. I'm on solid bedrock, and the bristles of my brush are like hamster fur. All of Jurassic Park could be directly below me, and I'd never get close—not without dynamite.

We stop for lunch, which takes place at the food truck in the parking lot.

"How does it feel to be where the action is?" Dr. Yee, Andrew's mother, asks me as we accept our hot dogs.

Action? Is that what paleontologists call this?

We only break for about fifteen minutes. Dr. Yee explains that this is because the days are getting shorter, so we have to make the most of the daylight hours. She seems really pumped up about it. The only way these scientists can keep their sanity is by convincing themselves that they're on the verge of an earth-shattering discovery.

So back I go to my paintbrush and my solid rock. As cold as the day is, the sun is warm, and I lie on my back to soak up its rays. I'm half-asleep when the commotion reaches me. Scientists are rushing toward the edge of the clearing, where a couple of them are struggling to pull something out of the ground. Something *big*.

I get up and run like everybody else, my heart pounding in sudden excitement. I understand now. The hours are long, but the moments, when they come, are spectacular. They are uncovering part of an animal that's been lost for a hundred million years or more!

"What is it?" I gasp. "A leg bone? A rib?"

"It's nothing," Dad says, his voice dripping with disappointment.

"But the *size* of it!" I exclaim. "Whatever dinosaur it's from, it must have been a big one!"

My father shakes his head. "Take a closer look, Dana. It's too straight. It's not a bone; it's modern lumber. We've been finding pieces like it for a couple of weeks now."

I stare at the "find." He's right. It seems like an old two-by-four, discolored, mud-encrusted, and partially decayed. "Why is it black?" I ask.

"Scorch marks." My father flakes off some of the dark shell with his chisel, revealing blond wood underneath. "There must have been a small building up here that burned, and they buried the debris. We've just been throwing them in the woods."

"Can I see the other pieces?" I feel stupid telling a bunch of PhDs that they don't know what they're looking at, but the fact is they don't. When you're searching for hundred-million-year-old bones, you don't waste your time on burnt two-by-fours. You don't bother to think about what those two-by-fours might mean.

Dad leads me to the edge of the clearing. Just inside the trees, there are seven or eight planks in a similar burnt condition. If this used to be some kind of building, surely it wouldn't be made of only two-by-fours. I step into the underbrush for a closer look. Each board has nail holes about three-quarters of the way up. On a couple of them, you can still see the stub of a crosspiece, burned black.

"Be careful, Dana," my father warns me. "There are nails in there."

I ignore him. "Dad, don't you know what this is? Don't you realize what you found?"

The response is a semicircle of blank stares.

"These are crosses!" I exclaim. "Burnt crosses! Don't you get it? This is the Night of a Thousand Flames—what's left of it anyway!"

Dad's eyes widen in surprise that gives way to some embarrassment. "How could we have missed that?"

"When you're looking for a dinosaur, you automatically ignore everything that isn't it," I tell him.

Dr. Yee has an important question. "Who do we call about

this? It's a find—even if it isn't *our* find. It's a piece of history. People should know about it."

My father cocks an eyebrow at me. "How about your friend ReelTok? He isn't very nice, but you have to admit that, when it comes to getting the word out, he's the expert."

"No!" I'm shocked at the wave of anger that surges through me. "ReelTok is the worst person on Earth! Do not give that creep a scoop! The way he used this town to push his YouTube channel, I want him to be the *last* to know!"

Dad produces his phone. "I'm calling Sheriff Ocasek. When word of this gets out, we'll need security to protect our dig from souvenir hunters. This is going to be big news!" He throws an arm around me and pulls me close. "Nice catch, kiddo! When did you get so smart?"

The light is fading, and the other scientists have all gone home by the time we get the okay from Sheriff Ocasek to head back into town.

"I'll keep a man out here until the university can hire its own security for the dig," the sheriff promises. "Strictly speaking, it isn't a crime scene."

"Forty years is a long time," Dad agrees.

Ocasek sighs. "Not sure it was considered a crime forty years ago either. It should have been, but it wasn't. I've been hearing about this ever since I was a little kid, younger than your daughter. My parents used to talk about it in hushed whispers so I wouldn't hear. I'd just about convinced myself it was a myth. And here we are."

"Times have changed," my father offers. "Chokecherry's a good town."

"I hope you're right," the sheriff says. "These last few weeks, I've seen things I never thought I'd see."

"You mean the swastikas in the school," I put in.

Ocasek nods sadly. "George Rowley's kid. The Bynes girl. Who knew?"

"There's the paper chain," my father points out. "Nobody would have predicted that either."

"I'll give you that," the sheriff agrees. "That's pretty special. Not sure what we're going to do with it, but what an achievement."

Sheriff Ocasek is one of those people who doesn't show much emotion—like he's seen it all, so nothing really impresses him anymore. But there's a brightness to his expression when he talks about the paper chain. I keep picturing his face as we drive home. I can't quite put my finger on it, but it's somewhere between pride and hope.

As we pull into the driveway, Dad says, "Well, we didn't find any fossils, but I think I'd call this a productive day, wouldn't you?"

Our headlights illuminate Ryan on the front porch, pushing a toy bulldozer. There, on his hands and knees, playing right along with my brother, is someone I never thought would have the nerve to show up at our house in a million years.

Link.

My father sizes up the murder in my eyes in a split second and hits the power locks before I can leap out the passenger door.

"Dana—be nice."

"Nice?" I spit. "To him? Why?"

"For starters, because Ryan is there."

"Fine, I'll send Ryan inside, and then I'll give that jerk the boot." I unlock the door manually, storm up the walk, and climb the two steps to the porch.

At the sight of me, Link jumps to his feet. He looks scared, which is exactly how he should be. He knows what's coming and how much he deserves it.

Ryan breaks the standoff. "Hi, Dana! We're playing trucks!"

My father sweeps ahead of me on the porch steps, grabs Ryan by the hand, and pulls him into the house with a curt "Link," in our visitor's direction. It isn't warm and welcoming, but it's a lot nicer than what I have planned.

But when the moment is upon me, I clam up. There are so many creative words I want to hurl at him that I can't decide which one to scream first. Plus, I'm afraid that Dad is lurking just inside the door, waiting to hear what I'm going to say so he can ground me for a hundred years.

Link raises his arms. "I know. I get it."

"You know *zilch*," I seethe. "If you think you can just say sorry and everything resets to zero, you're even more clueless than you must have been when you painted that swastika!"

He's shamefaced. "It's not that. I know you can never forgive me. I can't really forgive myself. There's no excuse for what

I did. I could tell you that I'm not the same person as I was back then, but I'm not even sure that's true."

I should be yelling. Instead, my voice is barely audible. "So why did you do it?"

He shrugs. "It was the worst thing I could think of. And even then I didn't really understand how awful it was. Not until the tolerance education unit—and by then it was too late."

"Not too late to go to Brademas and confess," I remind him.

He studies his sneakers. "I was scared. I know what people say about me. Stuck-up jock, thinks he can get away with anything. I was already in trouble for the fertilizer thing and half a dozen other stupid stunts. Nobody was ever going to believe that I did the first swastika, but not all the others. My dad pulled me out of sports over a little bit of lard on the road. I figured he'd disown me for this."

"So you lied to everybody," I accuse.

For the first time, Link looks as if he's about to give me an argument. Then he nods wearily. "You're right. I wasn't honest with people. And before I knew it, the paper chain was taking off, and if I told the truth, it might have tanked the whole thing."

I'm not any less furious, but I can appreciate his dilemma. The paper chain belonged to everybody, but he was almost the poster boy for it. If Link had spilled his guts, it would have ruined everything. It's still no excuse, but it's easy to see how it all got away from him.

I fold my arms in front of me. "So if you're not here to beg for forgiveness, what are you here for?"

"To tell you that the bar mitzvah is still on," he replies. "I confessed the whole thing to Rabbi Gold, and he was really cool about it. I know you can't come anymore—I don't expect you to. But I wanted to let you know it was happening, because I really couldn't have done it without your help."

After the revelation about the first swastika, I didn't think I could ever be surprised again about Link. But this stops me in my tracks. He's *having* the bar mitzvah? Seriously?

He picks up on my amazement. "I get how weird it is. Still, how could I not after what I learned about my grandmother? Her whole family was wiped out by the Nazis and I'm the guy who drew the first swastika? It'll never make that right, but I have to do *something*."

He's 100 percent sincere, blinking constantly, like he's trying not to cry. When the truth came out about what he did, I assumed that every word he'd told me was an out-and-out lie. That the whole thing—the grandmother, his heritage, the bar mitzvah—was just the latest and most elaborate of the series of unfunny pranks that he and his idiot friends are famous for. Like the fertilizer in the mail slot on a much larger scale.

But now the joke's over . . . and it turns out it was never a joke at all. That he was always working toward a bar mitzvah because he wanted one. And he still wants one in spite of everything that's happened and the fact that nobody's going to go to it.

I gawk at him. "You mean all that stuff about your grandmother—that's *true*?"

He stares at me in shock like I've just slapped him. Then

his shoulders slump and the rest of him deflates like a balloon. "Yeah, I get it," he tells me in a quiet voice. "I guess I don't deserve any better." He steps off the porch and disappears into the night.

I'm standing in front of my door feeling like I just kicked a friendly dog. Unbelievable! *He* painted the swastika, and *I'm* the one buried in guilt!

He's having a bar mitzvah because that's what Jewish kids do.

"Mazel tov, Link," I whisper into the darkness. "I hope you find a way to earn it."

CHAPTER THIRTY-ONE

LINCOLN ROWLEY

Dana once told me that the worst night of her life was the night before her bat mitzvah. She barely slept a wink, and when she finally did doze off, she was haunted by nightmares about forgetting her part, breaking an ankle in her high heels, and making an idiot out of herself in front of everybody she knew.

I don't have to worry about any of that. I won't be wearing high heels. And as for making an idiot out of myself, I took care of that long before the bar mitzvah could even get started. There's something about hitting bottom. The one thing you can be sure of is that things can't possibly get any worse and the only direction is up. I could mangle every single word of my Torah portion and I wouldn't let down anybody's expectations. Who would dare to expect anything but absolute zero from a painter of swastikas? And as for humiliating myself in front of people—what people? The only non-strangers who will be there are Mom, Dad, Grandma, and Grandpa. If I did the whole thing in Norwegian instead of Hebrew, they'd never know the difference.

Even if it hadn't come out that I painted that swastika, I don't think anybody in town would be in the mood to drive to Shadbush Crossing for a bar mitzvah tomorrow. Chokecherry is pretty embarrassed by the discovery of all those burnt crosses.

The Night of a Thousand Flames. No one can claim that it never happened now—not with the scientists digging up the final evidence. So half the town is embarrassed and sulking, not to mention ticked off at the other half, who are wagging their fingers to say *I told you so*. Everybody's in such a weird mood that they're ignoring the six-million-link paper chain that's stashed all around town. Probably the greatest achievement in Chokecherry history, and we're treating it like a dirty little secret.

Dad might be the unhappiest of all. Instead of digging up spectacular dinosaurs to put our town on the map, the Wexford-Smythe paleontologists are digging up proof that we're not worthy of an anthill, much less the theme parks and golf resorts that will make us the next Orlando. At this point, I think he's actually grateful to have a bar mitzvah to distract him from the fact that his dream of Dino-land is circling the drain.

And guess who's making sure the whole world knows about it—ReelTok. He's still here, minding everybody's business and vlogging his head off. He even claims he's coming to my bar mitzvah tomorrow. I have no idea how he found out it's still on. Maybe TokNation really does have members everywhere—including inside Temple Judea of Shadbush Crossing, Colorado. He's not allowed to livestream the service like he originally planned, because Rabbi Gold won't let him. But we can't keep him out. A synagogue is no different from a church or any house of worship—open to anybody.

Dad offered to drop the chamber of commerce lawsuit if he'd just go away, but no dice. That's something Dana didn't have to worry about on her big day: a vlogger in the audience waiting for her to make a mistake so he can blab about it to millions of followers.

She was right about the not sleeping part, though. I'm lying in bed, wired and wide-awake. I'm nervous about my performance, sure, but that's only a small part of it. Who would've believed it was possible to feel bad about so many things at the same time? Like the swastika I painted, and all the ones Pamela drew, because she was inspired by mine. And the role I played in creating the funk that hangs over the town like a fog. And the undeniable truth that my swastika brought ReelTok down on our heads. And the fact that Dad's dino dreams are probably never going to happen. They might not have happened anyway, but I definitely didn't help.

And then there's letting down Dana. She didn't want to help me at first. Why should she—it's not like any of us locals went out of our way to make the egglets feel welcome. But she did it anyway, because she's nice. She didn't give up on me, even though I knew as much about being Jewish as I know about building a nuclear power station out of Popsicle sticks. The moment I started to believe in myself was the moment I saw Dana starting to believe in me. And how do I repay her? Well, everybody already has the answer to that question.

It seems like a million years ago that I was an ordinary kid who thought nothing was more important than some upcoming sports season and my next dumb prank with Jordie and Pouncey. I barely even noticed the scientists' kids, and Jewish was something somebody else was in places far away from Chokecherry. I'm not sure I was happier then, but my life was a lot less complicated.

I get out of bed, pad to the window, and peer out into the

darkness. It's the same town I've known for thirteen years, but I'm a stranger in a strange land.

A lone snowflake dances past the window, wafting on an air current. I watch it, wondering if I'll ever truly be home again.

I wake up after a fitful night to the sound of urgent whispering on the other side of the door. My parents, engaged in the world's quietest argument.

"Let the poor kid sleep. There's nothing anybody can do about it now."

"We have to tell him. He'll find out eventually."

I roll out of bed and swing my legs to the floor. "Tell me what?"

That's when I tap my phone screen and get the shock of my life. It's 7:18! We were supposed to be on the road to Shadbush Crossing almost *twenty minutes ago*!

"We're late!" I wheeze in a panic.

"We're not late—" comes my mother's voice.

I cut her off. "I have to shower! And put on my suit! And tie the tie—you know it takes forever to get the tie!"

Dad comes into the room and wordlessly raises the blinds.

The world outside my window looks nothing like it did eight hours ago. You know that snowflake I saw last night? Well, it had about a gazillion babies. The first big storm of the winter must have started right after I went to bed. Chokecherry is buried under at least two feet of fresh snow.

I'm babbling. "We can still make it! You have an SUV! Those drive in snow, right?"

Dad shakes his head sadly. "Not *this* much snow. And it's even deeper in the mountains. The passes are all closed. No one is going anywhere."

Mom has a suggestion. "Maybe the rabbi will let us reschedule for next weekend."

"That's not how bar mitzvahs work!" I explain in agitation. "The part I learned from the Torah—that's only good for today. If we postpone till next Saturday, that means I spent all this time studying the wrong thing!"

Eventually, Dad gets us all calmed down enough to put a call through to Rabbi Gold.

The rabbi is out of breath when he comes on the line. "Sorry to keep you waiting, Lincoln. I was outside, shoveling."

I'm stunned. "Rabbis shovel?"

He sounds amused. "Moses parted the Red Sea. I'm not nearly as talented when it comes to my driveway."

"Rabbi," I exclaim, "the roads are all closed! I can't get there!"

His response is no help at all. "Our people have an old saying. It translates to 'Man makes plans and God laughs.' This is a perfect example of what it means. We made our plans. We did everything right. The one thing we can't control is the weather."

"Yeah, but what are we going to *do*?" I howl.

"That's the whole point of the saying," he explains patiently. "Try as we might, some things are beyond our capacity to change."

I'm almost in tears. "But I wanted it *so much*." The instant the words are out of my mouth, I realize that they're 100 percent true. Now that it's all falling apart, I want it more than I've ever wanted anything in my whole life.

The long silence on the other end of the line makes me feel even worse than I already do.

"Perhaps," the rabbi says thoughtfully, "we've been shown a way."

I'm stunned. "You mean, like, a miracle?"

"Not precisely. But if the phone lines work, chances are the internet does too. We can have this bar mitzvah *virtually*. We bring the synagogue into your living room via Zoom. And we can set up a screen so our congregation can watch you."

"And that's legal?" I blurt. "You know, Jewishly?"

"Well, it isn't in the Bible," he admits. "You won't find too many references to Zoom in the Torah. But if our modern age offers us a way for you to join our congregation today, we should be grateful for it. It may not be an official miracle, but it's a miracle of technology."

For the first time since Dad raised the blinds, I allow myself to hope. Okay, it isn't what I planned. I pictured myself at Temple Judea, surrounded by family and friends. Now Grandma and Grandpa won't even be able to get here through the mountains. They booked a hotel in Shadbush Crossing so they wouldn't get snowed out . . . and now they're snowed *in*.

On the other hand, has *anything* gone according to plan in my life lately? Not since I put that swastika on the wall. If you go by what I deserve, this makeshift Zoom-bar-mitzvah-buried-in-snow is more than I ever could have hoped for. Not only am I going to take it; I'm going to be grateful.

Rabbi Gold and I set it all up. I was supposed to be called to the pulpit at Temple Judea at 10:15, so that's when I have to be dressed and ready in the living room. The rabbi wants the Zoom connection to be online and running before the service starts so no one has to fiddle with electronics during a Sabbath service. I help Mom and Dad move some of the furniture around—it won't look great if the entire congregation of Temple Judea sees me tripping over an ottoman and knocking myself unconscious.

As we work, we detect signs of life outside our bay window—a plow clearing the main road, the scrape of shovels up and down the street, the spinning tires of a stuck car, the shouts of little kids having a snowball fight.

Dad and I drag in a high cocktail table to use as a podium— I have to be standing when I do my part. We put my laptop on a nearby shelf, and make sure that I'm on camera. Dad brings all these extra lamps down from the attic, until our living room is glowing like a TV studio.

"It's fine, Dad," I tell him. "It doesn't have to be perfect. They just have to be able to see me."

He's stubborn. "Any son of mine who's having a Zoom bar mitzvah is going to have the best Zoom bar mitzvah it's possible to have."

Honestly, seeing my father supporting me like this after everything that's happened makes me feel almost human again.

Then he ruins it: "Days like today. Problem-solving, thinking on your feet, dealing with the unexpected—these are the life skills that will help you find success in your future."

Barf.

We pause for a quick breakfast and scramble to get dressed for the main event. The tailor would be proud of me. Here it is, December 4, and I didn't have a growth spurt. I ruined my life fifteen different ways, but the suit still fits perfectly. It takes me four tries to get the tie on, and Dad still redoes it when he sees me.

"You look beautiful!" Mom says with a catch in her voice.

Ding-dong!

I experience a moment of excitement. I know it can't be Jordie, since he's banned from me. But maybe Pouncey managed to drag himself through the snow to support me. He probably thinks the bar mitzvah is off, and he's here to offer consolation. Still, it'll be great to have one friend on hand—assuming Pouncey can get through it without trying to make me laugh.

Dad has another theory. "Must be some kid trying to make money shoveling driveways."

My heart sinks. Dad's probably right. I did it myself last winter. "I'll get rid of him."

Trying to ignore the squeeze of my starched collar, I head downstairs and throw open the front door.

It isn't a kid with a shovel. It isn't even Pouncey. It's the last person I expect to see at this moment.

Dana Levinson.

"Good. You're dressed," she says briskly.

I start to explain about the plan-B Zoom bar mitzvah. Dana leans in past me and calls, "Mr. and Mrs. Rowley—we're in a hurry."

I look beyond her to the SUV parked in the driveway. It has heavy snow tires and a plow attachment in front. The Wexford-Smythe University crest is painted on the door. Dana's parents are in the front seat, and I can see Ryan in the back.

"What's this about?" I ask. "I have to be on Zoom at ten fifteen."

"Change of plan," she informs me. "Get your coat on. It's freezing out here."

I'm starting to get annoyed. "Aren't you listening? Because of the weather, I'm doing my bar mitzvah by video chat."

"That's still on. It's just been switched to the school, that's all. I called Rabbi Gold. He's totally on board."

I don't get it. "Why would I want to do this at the school? I don't even go there anymore."

"When you have a bar mitzvah," she lectures, "you're supposed to be surrounded by the people who care about you. They won't fit in your house."

"Aren't you forgetting something?" I snap. "These days, the people who care about me would fit in a phone booth and still leave room for the guy talking on the phone."

Mom and Dad appear at my side. They have their coats on, and my father hands me mine.

"We just got off the phone with Rabbi Gold," Mom supplies, pushing my bar mitzvah folder into my arms. "He explained the whole thing."

"Which is what?" My voice is rising.

"We're moving everything to the school," Dad tells me. "Don't worry, we'll have plenty of time if we hurry."

"How come I'm the only person who doesn't understand what's going on?" I complain. "I'm the one having the bar mitzvah."

I shrug into my coat, and we all pack up our shoes and kick into snow boots. Dana hustles us out to the SUV.

I'm a little nervous getting into the truck and facing the Levinsons. After all, I'm Swastika Guy. But for some reason, they seem happy to see me.

Dana's mother wishes me "Mazel tov."

"You must be so excited," her father adds.

"Thanks for inviting me to your bar mitzvah," Ryan pipes up. "You're invited to mine too. It's in six and a half years."

Mom and I end up squashed in next to Dana in the third row. "I understand it was you who put all this together," Mom says to Dana.

"She sure did," says Dr. Levinson behind the wheel. "Ever since she got up and saw the snow, she's been driving the whole town crazy. She's a born event planner."

"Yeah, but what event?" I whine. "Me Zooming the temple? Why does that have to happen at the school?"

Dana smiles the almost smile of the *Mona Lisa*. "You'll see."

The town roads have been plowed, so we have no trouble crossing Chokecherry. I can't help noticing that, the closer we get to the school, the busier the roads seem to be. That's unusual for the morning after a blizzard, when everybody stays home, drinking hot chocolate, and if you go out, it's for sledding, or maybe building a snowman.

When the school comes into view, I leap to my feet, smashing my head into the roof of the SUV. The place hasn't been this crowded since the championship game of the basketball tournament last spring. Mr. Kennedy is in the school district's mini tractor, plowing the parking lot to admit an endless stream of cars.

"What are all these people doing here?" I blurt, mystified.

"They're coming to a bar mitzvah," Dana replies. "Duh."

"Mine?" Nobody bothers to reply to that. There are no other bar mitzvahs happening at Chokecherry Middle School today. There probably hasn't been a bar mitzvah in this town since the beginning of time.

I try a different tack. "But how did everybody know about it? *I* didn't even know about it!"

"I have my methods," she says evasively.

We avoid the traffic jam in the parking lot and pull around the circular drive right up to the front entrance. We get out and join the river of people heading into the building. A lot of eyes are on me, but my eyes are riveted to a section of brick wall above the double doors. If I had X-ray vision, I'd be looking right through it at the atrium wall where I first spray-painted that swastika. Why are all these people coming to my bar mitzvah when everybody knows full well what I did?

There's a commotion ahead of us. Right at the doorway stands Sheriff Ocasek, blocking the way of a short pudgy man with a tripod resting on his shoulder.

"But I'm *invited*," ReelTok is trying to explain. "The Rowleys have agreed to let me livestream the ceremony to TokNation!"

"Sorry," the sheriff says gruffly. "My orders are to keep you out."

"Orders from *who*?" the vlogger demands, his unibrow arching into a V shape.

"From me," Ocasek replies. "I'm the law around here. I didn't like you before, and I like you even less now that I know you're only here to make trouble for this decent little town."

Now that he's at full outrage, Adam Tok looks very much like he does during his famous rants on YouTube. "Hasn't the news about freedom of the press made it to Chokecherry, Colorado?" He scans the crowd indignantly until his eyes light on Dana. "*She's* the one who invited me! Tell him, Dana!"

She smiles sweetly. "I didn't invite him. I just told him because I knew he would blab about it to his followers. It was the fastest way to spread the word to the whole town."

I gawk at her. "That's how you got everybody to come? By telling *him*?"

She beams. "It worked, didn't it?"

The sheriff addresses the vlogger. "There's a park across the street. You probably remember it. Maybe it's not too late to get your tent back."

Then ReelTok spots me. "Link—I know we haven't always seen eye to eye. But I've been *good* for you. I've been good for this town. The publicity that comes from millions of followers is pure gold. That doesn't have to be over! Think what the power of TokNation could mean for your future!"

I pull up short. It drives me crazy when my own father—who loves me—harps on my future. To hear it coming from this *sleazoid* puts me over the edge.

I round on the vlogger. "Mr. Tok, you did exactly one thing

that was good for me. You told the whole world what I did and that forced me to face it myself. So thanks for that, and please don't take it personally when I tell you where you can stick your millions of followers."

My folks and the Levinsons close in around me, and together we sweep past the sheriff and the vlogger into the school.

I've walked into that building hundreds of times before, but nothing could prepare me for what's laid out before me now.

The school is gone. Oh, I know it's still here, but the walls have been replaced by a supernova of color. Every single surface is hung with loops of red, orange, yellow, green, blue, purple, and every imaginable shade in between. For an instant, I'm so dazzled by the sheer impact of it that I can't put two and two together and figure out what it is.

A little gasp comes from my mother. "Link! It's—"

"The paper chain," I half whisper.

As we make our way through the halls, it's literally every-where. There are no walls, no windows, no lockers, no doorways. Mr. Brademas has to scissor his way into his own office. I'm a little nervous about meeting him. Even though it's the weekend, I'm still kicked out of this place. But he greets me warmly and even says, "Welcome back, Lincoln. I talked to your rabbi and I know you want to make amends. This is your chance."

We're inching along the corridor, rubbernecking, unwill-ing to miss a single link. It seems to go on forever, down every hall and up every stairwell.

Awestruck, I turn to Dana. "*You* did all this?"

"I called Caroline," she replies. "She rallied the troops.

Practically every kid came in to help us. Michael was the job foreman. Parents drove back and forth to the warehouses, picking up loads of chain. The whole town pitched in."

"Is this all of it?" I ask in amazement. "You know, all six million links?"

"Every single one," she confirms. "We even brought in everything from the silo. Mayor Radisson drove the city plow out there himself."

Up till now, there's been a fantasy quality about all this, but hearing names like Michael and Caroline makes everything very real. It raises a lump in my throat the size of a bowling ball, and I start to wonder if I'm going to be able to mumble a whole bar mitzvah past it.

As we turn the corner to the auditorium, a group of kids burst in from the faculty parking lot. They are laden with chain, multicolored strands wrapped around waists, arms, shoulders, and even necks.

"We almost forgot the Vardis' attic!" a girl calls to Dana. Then, spying me, the group races off ahead of us, amid stage whispers of "It's him!" and "Link's here!"

The auditorium is packed with people and blazing with color. Kids are everywhere, taping paper chain to the walls, and custodians are atop tall ladders, covering the higher, harder to reach places.

The Levinsons take my parents to special reserved seats in the front row. That leaves me totally alone—the focus of every eye. With the chairs in the orchestra pit, our auditorium seats over six hundred, and there are people packed into the aisles, and rows of standees at the back. Have you ever kicked out of snow boots and into shoes with a giant crowd watching? At least I can't fall. It's too crowded.

My bar mitzvah folder under my arm, I edge my way to the stage. There's a podium up there waiting for me and also a computer to provide the Zoom connection. It's the loneliest walk I've ever taken in my life. It reminds me of something Dana once told me—that the true purpose of a bar mitzvah is to make you so terrified that no matter what happens later in life, it won't be the most scared you've ever been. Finally, I understand what she meant. I could go swimming with great white sharks and it wouldn't compare to this.

I set my folder on the podium and turn my attention to the computer screen. It's my first ever look at Temple Judea of Shadbush Crossing, other than the inside of Rabbi Gold's office. It's smaller than I expected but nice, with stained-glass windows and rows of polished wooden pews. I wrap my tallit around my shoulders and put on my favorite kippah—the one with the logo of the Denver Broncos. At first I was afraid it was too un-Jewish, but Rabbi Gold assured me it's fine.

Speaking of Rabbi Gold, he's right there, beaming at me from the screen. The time is 10:15 on the nose. I know this is a religious ceremony, but the phrase that pops into my head comes from the Indy 500: *Gentlemen, start your engines . . .*

"Good morning, Lincoln," the rabbi greets me. "Before we get started, I have some people who'd like to say hello to you."

Two white-haired figures lean into the frame—Grandma and Grandpa!

"You made it!" I blurt.

"It takes more than a little snow to stop these two old fogies," Grandpa declares heartily.

"We're so sorry we can't be there in person," Grandma adds. "But we weren't going to miss this. We're so proud—" Her voice catches for an instant. "*I'm* so proud of you for what you're doing." My grandma, now an old woman but once a helpless baby, handed over into safety by her doomed parents.

Rabbi Gold ushers someone else into view. It's a man a little younger than Grandma and Grandpa, with a mustache and a shock of gray hair. In his arms, he carries a very old Torah scroll, the simple fabric of its cover threadbare and torn. "My name is Milton Friedrich. My father was a young soldier when he found this Torah in a Belgian village he helped liberate in 1944. It's been in my family all this time. We've always known it was important, but we've never known quite what to do with it—until we heard your story. And yours," he adds to Grandma.

On the screen, Grandma lets out a sniffle of emotion. I look down from the stage and see Mom dabbing at her eyes with a handkerchief in the front row.

"We've come an awfully long way," Mr. Friedrich goes on. "I'm sorry the weather has left some distance between you and our Torah. But we'll use it to follow along as you perform your bar mitzvah. And as soon as the roads clear, we'll bring it to you in Chokecherry to display beside the remarkable memorial of your paper chain."

As nervous as I am, I pick up my laptop, turn it around,

and pan the room with its webcam, giving Temple Judea a view of the big auditorium, hung with miles of paper chain. "This is only a fraction of it," I say. "It's all here, filling the whole school. Three hundred seventy-eight miles of it, according to Michael Amorosa—and he's never wrong."

The rabbi's voice is husky. "All six million links?"

We've gotten kind of used to the paper chain, but I'm suddenly seeing it through Rabbi Gold's eyes—every single loop commemorating a life lost but not forgotten. Who would understand that better than a rabbi?

"Every single one," I confirm.

Rabbi Gold takes a long moment to get himself together while I set the laptop back in place on the podium. Then he starts the service, and before you know it, I'm on.

But something feels wrong. I'm not ready to start yet. I'm standing before my friends, my classmates, and a pretty fair chunk of my town—a town I plunged into a lot of hassle with my stupid, thoughtless actions. Before I start chanting at them in a language they don't understand, I owe them something important—in plain English.

"Rabbi Gold?" I ask. "I know this is a strange request, but would it be okay if I do the speech part first?"

He peers at me intently, and even over Zoom, I can tell he understands why I need to do this.

He nods. "Very well."

I've already written a speech as part of my bar mitzvah. It's about Jacob and Esau, whose story my Torah reading covers. But that's not the speech I'm planning to give. I'm going to have to wing this one. And I'd better get it perfect, because nothing I've ever said is this important.

"In the past few days," I begin, "I've said the words *I'm sorry* more times than I ever thought I would in my whole life. I won't make excuses, because there are none. The best I can do is say it one more time. I'm so, so sorry.

"The fact that you're here means everything to me. Because of what I did, there's been a lot of negative attention on our town. Some of that comes from stuff that happened a long time ago, and some comes from stuff that's more recent. But we also got something great—our paper chain, six million links long, which is all around us. I hope it proves that, when we work together, it's possible to take some of the bad and turn it into good.

"Today, I will become the first bar mitzvah in my family since my grandmother's father—a man she never even knew. He was killed in the Holocaust, so if this isn't a chance to turn bad into good, I don't know what is. The Nazis tried to cut off my family line. With your support, I'm here to show that it's still going."

I shake my head. "I'm not sure I'm worthy of something that huge. I know what I did was unforgivable. I'd give any-thing to be able to change it, but that's not how the world works. We can't change the past. All we can do is work hard to make things right in the future. I promise that, for me, that starts now."

And with a deep breath, I launch into my bar mitzvah.

At the beginning, my voice comes out higher than I expected, and the Hebrew words sound alien, the way they did when I first started trying to learn all this. I know a new kind of dread—one that has nothing to do with how badly I've messed up my life in the past few weeks. Dana warned me about this. It's something all bar and bat mitzvah kids share: a paralyzing fear of making a fool out of yourself in front of everybody you know and quite a few that you don't.

For an instant, it's like I'm hovering above my own body, watching the proceedings and wondering what's going on. How did Lincoln Rowley end up in *this* place, surrounded by *these* people, doing *this* thing?

Just as I'm about to fall apart, the endless hours of practice kick in and I'm sailing along in complete control. It's not so much that I know what I'm doing. It's more like autopilot. It's really strange. It starts as *Please don't let me mess this up*, but pretty soon, I'm not just surviving, I'm nailing it!

On the screen, I can see Rabbi Gold, following along and nodding his approval. In the front row, Mom's gaze is riveted on me. Dad clenches the arms of his seat, his knuckles white. A few seats away, Dana is beaming with pride, like she invented me or something.

A little farther back, Jordie is pumping his fist, like he's watching a soccer match and I'm on a breakaway. Next to him, Pouncey is making faces at me. Sophie has him by the ear, trying to get him to stop.

I see Michael in the control booth, regulating volume and lighting in the auditorium. His lips are moving, and I'm pretty sure he's mumbling along with me. I spent so much time practicing while paper-chaining that he learned my entire bar mitzvah by sheer repetition! Caroline is with him behind the glass, scanning the crowd like she considers herself the owner of the school, so these people are all her guests.

By this time, my confidence is soaring. As I head into the final prayer, even my voice has settled down to normal. I can't tell what's going on at Temple Judea, but in the auditorium at Chokecherry Middle School, you could hear a pin drop. I have plenty of experience being the center of attention—on a soccer field, a basketball court, a baseball diamond. That's nothing compared to hundreds of people hanging on your every word, even though they haven't got a clue what those words mean.

When I get to the final phrase—*M'kadesh hashabbat*—I really drag it out, my own personal opera. The Chokecherry crowd, who don't know any better, leap to their feet in a thunderous standing ovation. That's not supposed to happen. I don't know any better either, so I actually take a bow, totally thrilled with myself. Anyway, it can't be that wrong, because they're clapping at Temple Judea too.

Grandma's cheeks are streaked with tears. "Wonderful! Just wonderful!" She says more than that, but I don't have a hope of hearing it, because things are pretty loud in the auditorium.

Kids mob the front row, cheering and calling for me to stage dive. I catch a glimpse of my mother, waving her arms and shouting, "Don't you dare—"

That's all it takes. I don't dive, exactly, but I step off the edge and allow the forest of reaching arms to catch me. It isn't very bar mitzvah, but it wouldn't be me unless I did at least one stupid, impulsive thing. Hands high-five me and slap at my back and shoulders.

One of them belongs to Dad. He leans in and bellows into my ear, "I never should have worried about your future! The way you pulled that off—"

I miss the rest of it, because the kids bear me away. I haven't been carried since I was a toddler, and it's a weird feeling, bounce-rolling toward the auditorium exit with zero control over where I'm going.

"*Duck!*" Dana yells.

I flatten myself to the mob a split second before the low doorway would have taken my head off. Then I'm out in the hall, bobbing and weaving through walls of endless paper chain.

I manage a feeble "Hey, you guys, put me down," but I don't think anybody hears me. My crowd of bearers keeps growing. We're a tidal wave rolling through the school, with me like a tiny canoe being carried away on it. I'm actually starting to get a little seasick.

I struggle to make sense of the voices that are boiling up all around me.

"That was awesome, Link!"

"I don't know what it was, but you killed it!"

"You're getting another shot—don't blow it!"

"How did you learn all that? It isn't even in American!"

Jordie barks, "Best mitzvah ever!" Like he has anything to compare it to.

Pouncey adds, "You should have warned me it was going to be boring."

"The student council is proud of you!" Caroline pants up at me.

She's out of breath because the crowd is picking up speed in the hall, the paper chain walls blurring into a cascade of color. I peer ahead and see the front entrance, the sunlight reflecting brilliantly off the newly fallen snow. I'm starting to worry about where all this is going to end. Am I about to be hurled through a plate-glass window into a snowbank?

I try to roll free off the arms that are carrying me but succeed only in tearing a length of paper chain.

"Stop!" I'd know Michael's voice anywhere. "You're ripping the chain!"

They don't drop me—it's more like the group that's supporting me disintegrates and I get dumped on the floor as everyone rushes to fix the fallen links.

A hand yanks me back to my feet. Dana.

I brush off my suit. "So how'd I do?"

"It was . . . adequate," she replies before breaking into a big grin.

"I can't believe you did all this for me," I tell her honestly. "I can't believe everybody else went along with it. Not after I was such a jerk."

"We all do jerky things," she assures me. "It's what you do *next* that matters. What you did next inspired a lot of people."

That's when I realize that we're in the atrium, right at the base of the stairs. I gaze up at the blank wall, and for the first time in forever, I don't see the swastika I put there. Oh, sure, it's been washed off and painted away for months now.

But today, it's finally gone.

CHAPTER THIRTY-TWO

MICHAEL AMOROSA

Caroline is already bugging me to be her running mate when she goes for eighth-grade president next year. She says it's because I'm "the right person for the job," but I know she's just trying to glom off my reputation as the main guy behind the paper chain project. I'm more high-profile than ever now that the *Guinness Book of World Records* is coming to Chokecherry to photograph our chain for their new edition. In this town, if you need somebody who can count up to six million, I'm your man.

But I don't tell her any of that, even though it's true. I just say that I'm going to be busy enough as president of the art club next year.

Have you ever tried to say no to Caroline McNutt? It isn't easy.

"How can you pass this up for stupid art club?" she demands. "Not that art club is stupid. But in student government, you can change the *world*!"

"No, you can't," I tell her. "You can't even change the school unless Brademas gives the okay."

I'd never admit it to Caroline, but in a way, our student government really did change the world. The idea for the paper chain started at a student council meeting. And by the end of it, we had contributions from families and schools all around the globe. I can't even guess how many people we reached. It wasn't just ReelTok's millions of followers. The newspapers, TV stations, and media outlets that covered us probably brought our story to hundreds of millions more. We might be almost as famous as that school in Whitwell, Tennessee, and their paper clips project—and somebody made a movie about *them*.

And our paper chain isn't over yet. I mean, it's *done*—we've got our six million links. Nobody wants to try for thirty like they did in Tennessee. But the *impact* of the paper chain is just getting started. The Monday after Link's bar mitzvah, the town council votes unanimously to build a museum and tolerance center in Chokecherry. They've lined up the first three exhibits already. Number one is the paper chain, obviously. Number two is the Holocaust Torah that Mr. Friedrich drove down from Canada. And number three is the scorched timbers from the crosses that were burned around our town on the Night of a Thousand Flames. Technically, they're the property of the dinosaur dig, but Wexford-Smythe University donates them to the project. They're only interested in what happened a hundred million years ago. 1978 isn't paleo enough for them.

I'm amazed at how many community members are there to greet Mr. Friedrich and his wife when the mountain passes are finally open and he brings the Torah to Chokecherry. Link's bar mitzvah was more than a religious service; it really changed people around here.

Even Pouncey shows up. "Cool scroll. I mean, it's taken

more punishment than the whole town combined, and it's still in one piece. Plus, the next time some genius like Brademas decides we need tolerance education, we can just point to the new museum and tell him to back off."

"Admit it," Link chides him. "You liked paper-chaining just as much as anybody."

"The guillotine was pretty okay," he admits. "I miss it sometimes."

"You should join the art club," I suggest.

It's the wrong thing to say. The paper chain may have changed us, but I don't think I'm ever going to make it into that popular crowd. I'm okay with that. It feels pretty awesome to be me these days. Good things are happening . . . and I'm a part of it.

Another person who turns up to greet the Friedrichs is ReelTok, with his ever-present camera and tripod. It's a tricky moment for a whole town that's embracing tolerance, because most of us have trouble tolerating ReelTok. He used us to attract followers and made our town look so bad. Chokecherry may be no place for hate now, but we're willing to make an exception for a certain vlogger.

When ReelTok interviews Mr. Friedrich, he plays town hero, like none of this could possibly have happened without his glorious TokNation. I guess he's partly right. He stirred up a lot of trouble, but it created a ton of publicity for our paper chain. As much as I hate to admit it, he deserves some of the credit for our tolerance museum. He also deserves a punch in the nose. But, hey, that wouldn't be tolerant.

In my opinion, the most amazing thing about the tolerance museum is the fact that the burnt crosses are going to be a part of it. Remember, a couple of weeks ago, half the town didn't believe that the Night of a Thousand Flames ever happened. Still, the vote to include it was 100 percent yes. That's Chokecherry finally admitting its KKK past, even though people like Pouncey's grandfather and Pamela's great-uncle aren't around anymore. I haven't talked to the other minority kids about it—Dana, Andrew, maybe even Link. But to me, that's huge.

Speaking of Pamela, the word around town is her dad accepted a job in Colorado Springs and the family will be moving soon. It's kind of a relief, since she's the one person who it's really hard to forgive. What Link did was terrible, but it was mostly a stupid impulse. What she did—and how many times she did it—was with deliberate and evil purpose. Still, it doesn't seem right to heap all the blame on one person or one family. There's a history there too.

Maybe it shows that tolerance is more about the journey than the destination. A paper chain can be done when it hits a certain number of links. But tolerance is a project you always have to keep working at.

CHAPTER THIRTY-THREE

REELTOK

From the YouTube channel of Adam Tok

Interview with Lincoln Rowley—Final

REELTOK: Well, TokNation, our good work in Chokecherry, Colorado, is done. The paper chain is complete, and this once-unknown town has become a household word around the world. There's one thing left to do before we bid farewell to a grateful community—pay a visit to the bar mitzvah boy himself, Link Rowley. Just let me set up my tripod on the porch so I can ring the doorbell . . .

GEORGE ROWLEY: You've got some nerve coming here!

REELTOK: I have a few questions for your son before I ride off into the sunset.

GEORGE ROWLEY: He has nothing to say to you. The chamber of commerce dropped the lawsuit. The least you can do is go away.

LINK: It's okay, Dad. I'll talk to him.

GEORGE ROWLEY: We don't need to have anything more to do with this parasite.

LINK: I got this, Dad.

GEORGE ROWLEY: Okay . . . but I'll be just inside if you need me.

REELTOK: First of all, Link, congratulations on your bar mitzvah. Sorry I couldn't attend the service, but I had urgent business on behalf of TokNation.

LINK: You mean the urgent business of being kicked out by the sheriff?

REELTOK: Here's question one: In the Jewish faith, a bar mitzvah signifies the beginning of manhood. Do you feel like a man now?

LINK: How I feel is really, really lucky. I did pretty much the stupidest thing it's possible to do. And not stupid-funny. Stupid-awful. And everybody forgave me for it.

REELTOK: Do you believe you deserve forgiveness and Pamela doesn't?

LINK: You mean because my family turned out to be from the Holocaust and hers turned out to be from the KKK? She has no control over that. Why should I be let off the hook and not her? We both did the same thing. But I'm trying to change—to make things right. I hope she'll eventually do that too.

REELTOK: Are you a different person now?

LINK: I hate what I did. I'm humiliated by it and I'm

sorry it happened. But I'm still the same guy who painted that swastika.

REELTOK: Not a thunderous claim that you've turned over a new leaf.

LINK: I'm just being honest. I want to do better. I hope I'm smarter. I'm *trying*.

REELTOK: Fair enough. Final question: Are you Jewish now?

LINK: I'm exactly as Jewish as I was six months ago.

REELTOK: In other words, you're not Jewish.

LINK: I didn't say that. Technically, I'm a hundred percent—my grandmother, my mother, me. But I don't know how the rest of my life is going to go. Maybe that's why you have bar mitzvahs at thirteen— it's the perfect time to start exploring who you are. Like I was always this sports kid, but through the paper chain, I realized I could be friends with different kinds of people I never thought about much before. It wasn't the point of the paper chain, but it was a great side effect. It brought everybody together.

REELTOK: And it made your town famous . . . thanks to TokNation.

LINK: Fine. You spread the word about us—along with a lot of other stuff we could have lived without. Being famous has its downside.

REELTOK: You're speaking about how the publicity brought out Chokecherry's racist past. I'm sure your father isn't thrilled about that. With all this buzz about burning crosses and the KKK, his Dino-land plans must be pretty much dead. So much for making this town the next Orlando.

LINK: Hey, who needs that? With our new tolerance museum, we're going to be the next Whitwell, Tennessee!

AUTHOR'S NOTE

This novel would never have been possible without inspiration from the famous Paper Clips Project, by eighth graders from Whitwell Middle School in Whitwell, Tennessee. In 1998, in response to an after-school unit on the Holocaust, the students got the idea to collect six million paper clips to represent the six million Jewish victims of the Holocaust. They chose paper clips because the citizens of Norway wore paper clips to protest the Nazi occupation during World War II.

That project eventually became Whitwell's world-renowned Children's Holocaust Memorial, housed in an actual Nazi railcar that was once used to deport German Jews to the concentration camps. The car holds eleven million paper clips, representing the six million murdered Jews plus five million non-Jewish victims of the Nazi regime.

In the end, the students of Whitwell collected more than thirty million paper clips and inspired several books and at least two feature films. In this novel, when the students of Chokecherry embark on a tolerance education unit in response to the swastika defacing their atrium, there's no question that the remarkable accomplishments of their fellow middle schoolers in Tennessee would be among the first topics they'd study.

And as the racist vandalism continues, it makes perfect sense that the Chokecherry kids might try to follow in the footsteps of their Whitwell predecessors. Then they can begin to learn what the Paper Clips Project taught us all: that the first step in wrapping your mind around the unimaginably vast tragedy of the Holocaust is to wrap your mind around that unimaginably vast number of six million.

In this book, Michael Amorosa says, "A paper chain can be done when it hits a certain number of links. But tolerance is a project you always have to keep working at." Here are some of the many organizations and institutions that can provide resources in the fight against anti-Semitism, Holocaust denial, racism, and intolerance:

The Anti-Defamation League at ADL.org

The Southern Poverty Law Center at splcenter.org

The Museum of Jewish Heritage at mjhnyc.org

The USC Shoah Foundation Visual History Archive at sfi.usc.edu/collections/holocaust

The United States Holocaust Memorial Museum at ushmm.org, including their learning site for students at encyclopedia.ushmm.org/content/en/project/the-holocaust -a-learning-site-for-students